# Shark Attack!

Frank was just now paddling out from the shore. Joe held off for a few more waves and then positioned himself for the next group coming in.

"Hurry up!" Joe urged his brother, paddling into place. "This set's a winner!"

"Watch out!" came Frank's warning.

"I am watching," Joe said, his eyes on the coming waves.

The perfect wave was rolling up toward him. Joe was in just the right spot. He knelt on the board and got ready to stand.

But Frank had not been warning his brother about the waves.

"It's a shark!" Frank cried.

Joe clutched at his surfboard. In that split-second's hesitation, it was too late to grab the break. Joe steadied himself for the inevitable wipeout. As the wave tumbled over him in a spray of foam, the last thing he saw was a telltale fin—coming right at him!"

# The Hardy Boys Mystery Stories

## Available from MINSTREL Books

## 129

# *The* HARDY BOYS®

## THE TREASURE AT DOLPHIN BAY

FRANKLIN W. DIXON

A MINSTREL® BOOK

PUBLISHED BY POCKET BOOKS

New York   London   Toronto   Sydney   Tokyo   Singapore

This book is a work of fiction. Names, characters, places and incidents are products of the author's imagination or are used fictitiously. Any resemblance to actual events or locales or persons, living or dead, is entirely coincidental.

A MINSTREL PAPERBACK *Original*

A Minstrel Book published by
POCKET BOOKS, a division of Simon & Schuster Inc.
1230 Avenue of the Americas, New York, NY 10020

Copyright © 1994 by Simon & Schuster Inc.
Front cover illustration by Vince Natale

Produced by Mega-Books, Inc.

ISBN: 0-671-87213-3

First Minstrel Books printing December 1994

10  9  8  7  6  5  4  3  2  1

THE HARDY BOYS MYSTERY STORIES is a trademark of Simon & Schuster Inc.

THE HARDY BOYS, A MINSTREL BOOK and colophon are registered trademarks of Simon & Schuster Inc.

Printed in the U.S.A.

# Contents

# THE TREASURE
# AT DOLPHIN BAY

# 1 Swimming with the Dolphins

"Cowabunga!" Joe Hardy cried, jumping into the passenger seat of the four-wheel-drive jeep his brother, Frank, had rented. "Finally—the sun is out, there's not a cloud in the sky, and we get to do some sight-seeing."

"Of something more than the Hawaiian rain," Joe's older brother, Frank, agreed. Joe was seventeen and Frank was eighteen.

Frank put the jeep in gear. He drove away from the resort hotel where they were staying, along with their parents, Fenton and Laura Hardy. A week on the Hawaiian island of Maui had sounded like paradise to Frank and Joe. Unfortunately, they'd spent the first two days of their Christmas vacation in the hotel room, watching the rain come down. At last, the weather was clear and sunny. While their parents played a round of golf at the resort's championship course, Frank and Joe were headed to the nearby town of Nai'a Bay. There they planned to visit the Institute for Cetacean Studies, a world-famous center for the research of dolphins.

"It says here that a few visitors actually get to swim with the dolphins," Joe said, reading from a brochure in his hand. He'd picked up the pamphlet in the hotel lobby the night before.

"I know," said Frank. "You get into the lagoon with them, and they swim between your legs. You can even hold on to their fins and go for a ride."

"How did you know?" Joe asked.

"You've mentioned it only about five times," Frank said with a good-natured laugh.

He pulled the jeep into the late morning traffic. To their left the road curved along Maui's rugged coastline. Joe knew the mountains were actually volcanoes. The beach in front of their hotel was white sand, but it was surrounded on either side by sharp, black lava rock. To their right, the lush green fields of sugarcane rose gradually to meet the volcanic mountains. Joe put on his sunglasses while Frank cruised into the fast lane.

"Do you think I could become a dolphin researcher?" Joe wanted to know. He pored over the brochure. "There are pictures here of some of the people who work at ICS. They look pretty young."

Frank glanced over Joe's shoulder when they stopped at a red light. "I guess," he said. "But what about your career as a detective?"

2

Back home in Bayport, Frank and Joe were known as ace amateur detectives. They'd solved many cases in their hometown, and some on the road, too.

Joe grinned. "Don't worry, big brother. I won't desert the team. Not even for a bunch of dolphins."

He went back to reading the brochure while Frank followed the directions Joe had given him for Nai'a Bay. Soon they were turning off the main highway onto a two-lane road lined by towering coconut trees. On either side, thick flowering bushes hid rows of sugarcane from view. Straight ahead was the ocean, its shimmering blue surface marked by waves and foam.

When they got to the main street of Nai'a Bay, Joe saw that the town was no more than a half dozen blocks long. At one end, he spotted a pier and what looked like a scuba shop. At the other end of the curving shore was the dolphin center. In between was a supermarket, a movie theater, and several one-story buildings that had long, wide porches. From reading his parents' guidebook, Joe knew that Nai'a Bay had been a whaling town. In the secluded bay, several boats bobbed in the water at their moorings. Farther out, beyond the reef, Joe spotted some surfers catching the break in a wave. Not much farther than that, Joe noticed a small island that was shaped like a hat.

Frank turned the car left toward the dolphin center. Soon they were pulling into a nearly filled parking lot. The Institute for Cetacean Studies was a group of one-story buildings made of black lava rock and glass. Palm trees and flowering bushes surrounded the buildings.

"I guess the tourists have found this spot," Joe remarked as he and Frank got out of their four-by-four. Sure enough, the line to get into the museum and exhibition center was long. Frank and Joe waited for ten minutes before they were admitted. A sign at the ticket booth told them that the actual research center was only open for public visiting one day a week. Today was the day, which explained why the place was so crowded.

"Gee, only one person gets to swim with the dolphins," Joe remarked out loud.

"How do they choose who gets to do it?" Frank asked.

"They use a lottery system," Joe told his brother. "Everyone gets a number. At noon the winning ticket is chosen. Let's just hope mine is the lucky one!"

For the next hour, Frank and Joe made their way through the center's extensive museum and exhibition halls. They learned about the various breeds of dolphins, and how the mammals had been trained throughout history. They discovered that the scientists and researchers at ICS were the leading authorities on dolphin behavior, and ICS prided itself on its humane research. As they were watching a videotape of the experiments being done at ICS, Joe watched, transfixed.

"The people here have learned how to communicate with them," he whispered to Frank. "And the dolphins know how to respond to commands."

4

On the screen, a dolphin splashed playfully in the water. At the side of the lagoon, a scientist waved her arms in a series of gestures. The dolphin let out a loud noise that sounded almost like a bark and dove underwater. Ten seconds later, the dolphin reemerged with a hoop across its nose. The scientist rewarded the dolphin with a pat on the nose and a piece of fish.

"Awesome!" Joe exclaimed. "But I want to check it out for real."

It was almost time for the lottery drawing to take place. Visitors were moving from the museum and exhibition space to the area beside the lagoon. Bleachers were set up in a semicircle around one half of the lagoon. A line was forming at a ticket booth. Joe headed over to the booth while Frank found two seats.

"The dolphin looks like it's ready for some action," Frank said when Joe sat down beside him. The lagoon extended from the bleachers to a natural reef about three hundred yards away. A dolphin was frolicking in the lagoon. It jumped, making an arc in midair, then it whistled and squealed. A woman in a wet suit stood at the edge of the lagoon, giving the dolphin hand signals.

"I'd give anything to be picked," Joe said, his eyes following the action. He looked at the number on the ticket in his hand. "Thirteen," he groaned. "Talk about unlucky!"

After another minute or so, the woman stood before the crowd and announced, "I'm Maggie Cone, one of the trainers here at ICS. I know you're all eager to have your chance to swim with our dolphin, Kalea. He's going to pick a number from that basket by the side of the lagoon. Whoever holds a ticket with that number, please come forward." Maggie shot the crowd a quick smile. "Everyone ready?"

The crowd shouted out a loud "Yes!" Maggie made a series of hand gestures, and Kalea swam toward a basket at the far side of the lagoon. He dug his snout into the basket, and came up with a square piece of white plastic. Then he swam over to Maggie, who took the plastic piece from Kalea's mouth. She held it up and said, "My personal favorite unlucky lucky number is thirteen. Will the person with ticket number thirteen please stand up?"

"Joe," Frank cried. "That's you!" Frank pushed his brother out of his seat.

Joe Hardy couldn't believe it. He was glad he came prepared, wearing his swimsuit under his shorts. He quickly stepped out of his clothes and handed them to his brother. As he made his way down the bleachers, people gave him smiles and envious looks.

At the bottom, Maggie Cone stood waiting for him. When Joe saw her up close, he realized she was the trainer in the video he'd just seen. There was no mistaking her red-blond hair and her startlingly blue eyes. Maggie flashed Joe a grin, and then proceeded to count off instructions on her fingers.

"Stay calm and relaxed. Don't swim up to the dolphin. Let him come to you. If he pushes himself between your legs, that means he wants to take you for a ride. Hold on to his dorsal fin—do you know what that is?" she asked.

"You bet," Joe said. "The fin on his back."

"Exactly," Maggie said with a smile. She handed Joe a life vest, and watched him put it on. "Don't grip Kalea's fin too tightly. If he throws you off, don't fight it. Let him teach you. The lagoon is his environment and we are his guests. Remember that. Oh, and have fun!"

With that, Maggie led Joe to the edge of the lagoon. Joe tested the water with his toe and found it to be quite warm. He slid in and swam slowly away from the edge.

Trying not to hope for much, Joe treaded water in the warm, saltwater lagoon. Maggie had said Kalea might not be up for a swim. Joe spotted a plume of spray across the lagoon, and saw Kalea's tail slap the water playfully. Joe swam a few strokes in the direction of the mammal. From across the lagoon came the sound of Kalea's high-pitched whistles. At first, Joe thought he'd upset the dolphin. He looked over to Maggie for guidance.

"Good news," said Maggie. "That means he's ready to play."

Sure enough, Kalea came darting through the water, and suddenly Joe felt the dolphin's nose butting against his legs.

"Relax," Maggie called out. "You're doing fine."

Joe relaxed as Kalea pushed his nose between Joe's legs. In a flash, Joe was on top of the dolphin's smooth, wet body.

"Hold on!" Joe heard Frank call out.

Joe almost lost his balance, but a second later he found the fin on Kalea's back and used it to steady himself—just in time. The dolphin picked up speed, cutting through the water at a fast clip. Suddenly Kalea darted underwater, taking Joe with him. Then he went flying through the air, Joe still on his back.

"Wow!" Joe cried, going down for another dunk.

Kalea frolicked about with Joe on his back for nearly five minutes. Once, Joe fell off Kalea's back, but the mammal quickly made a U-turn, swam alongside, and picked him up again.

"How is it?" Frank shouted. He was now standing at the edge of the lagoon.

"Better than a roller coaster ride, that's for sure," Joe called back. "The only problem is, he's slippery!"

The crowd laughed, and Joe went back to concentrating on the ride. As Kalea started to pull him back out to the far end of the lagoon, Joe spotted Maggie giving the dolphin another series of signals.

"Time to come in," Maggie called out.

The scientist blew on a whistle several times, but still the dolphin wouldn't respond.

Maggie's voice became more insistent, and she blew on the whistle several more times. Joe didn't know what to do. Kalea was swimming—fast—for the reef. And he didn't seem about to respond to Maggie. Should he jump off, Joe wondered, or should he stay on?

There wasn't much choice. By now, Kalea was swimming so fast that Joe wasn't really able to get off.

"Take it easy," Joe said. Then he laughed. He knew what Frank would say: Dolphins may be smart, but they didn't exactly understand English.

Kalea let out a high-pitched squeal and then a whistle. Farther out in the water, Joe heard what he thought must be a reply. He heard the same squeal, and a lower whistle. Kalea whistled again. The low whistle came back to them. Joe scanned the reef, and realized suddenly what was making the sound. There was another dolphin out there!

Kalea continued to swim for the reef. As they got closer, Joe marveled at Kalea's intelligence. There was no way he as a human would have seen the other dolphin, let alone have heard it. But somehow Kalea had known.

Soon they were close enough for Joe to see. The other dolphin was on the other side of the reef, which emerged from the ocean floor and made a natural barrier between the lagoon and the ocean. Kalea pulled Joe closer, still calling to the other dolphin.

But something seemed to be wrong. The dolphin wasn't able to swim over the reef. Kalea must have sensed a problem, because she dropped Joe gently onto the reef. From his rocky perch in the shallow

9

water, Joe watched Kalea jump the reef, then nudge the other dolphin with his nose.

The dolphin looked as if it was having trouble breathing. In fact, it seemed as if it was barely alive. Kalea pushed the dolphin over the reef.

That's when Joe saw the bloody wound in the dolphin's side.

# 2 Kalea Saves
# the Day

Joe's mind raced. He knew he had to do something to help the dolphin, or else it might bleed to death.

But while Joe tried to think of what to do, Kalea had already swung into action. He nudged the other dolphin into the lagoon, and then leapt back over the reef. Joe, meanwhile, stood awkwardly on the reef and tried to signal Maggie and Frank, but they were too far away to see clearly. Realizing that he was on his own, Joe dove off the reef and prepared to swim back to shore. It would be a long haul, but he knew he could make it.

Kalea seemed to sense Joe's thoughts. Leaving the injured dolphin for a moment, Kalea whistled, squealed, and swam under Joe's legs. "Okay," Joe agreed, grabbing on to the dolphin's dorsal fin. "If you think you can handle us both. I didn't feel like making that swim anyway!"

On the way in to shore, Joe kept his eye on the injured dolphin. It couldn't swim on its own very well, and Kalea did a tremendous job of getting both the dolphin and Joe through the lagoon.

When Kalea, Joe, and the dolphin got back to the waiting crowd, Frank helped Joe out of the water, while Maggie crouched at the edge of the lagoon. "This is awful!" she said, getting a firsthand view of the dolphin's bloody wound. An older woman beside her showed concern on her tanned face.

"It's Poipu!" Maggie cried, looking up at the older woman.

"That dolphin is seriously hurt," the woman said, kneeling down beside Maggie.

By now, the ICS staff was swinging into action. A man and a woman, both wearing scuba gear, hopped into the lagoon to tend to the dolphin. Another ICS employee urged the curious crowd back to their seats in the bleachers. Meanwhile, a stocky boy with dark hair appeared at Joe's side.

"What happened?" he asked. The boy appeared to be Joe's age. He wore a blue T-shirt with the ICS logo on it and white shorts. "I'm Stan Ho'opi'i, an intern here. That's Dr. Helen Cho," he said, pointing to the older woman. "She's the head of ICS."

In her T-shirt, jeans, and sandals, Dr. Cho looked more like a student than a world-renowned dolphin researcher. But Joe knew from reading the brochure about ICS that Helen Cho was an expert in dolphin communication, and that she had single-handedly built ICS into what it was.

Joe quickly told Stan about his swim with Kalea, and how the mammal had rescued the injured dolphin. "Do you think he'll be okay?" Joe asked. He watched Dr. Cho, Maggie, and the two vets tend to Poipu.

Stan shrugged. "Let's hope so. Don—he's the head vet—really knows his stuff. As long as Poipu didn't lose a lot of blood, he should be okay."

The crowd was scattering now. By the lagoon, Dr. Cho and the vet were engaged in serious conversation. Joe was pretty sure he heard the words "speargun wound." He grabbed Frank's arm and told his brother what he'd overheard. With a surprised look on his face, Frank approached Stan. "Is it possible that someone shot at Poipu? Are the dolphins allowed to swim in open water alone?" he asked.

"They are," Stan confirmed. He rubbed his hands along his thick, muscular arms. "They're free to swim wherever they want, whenever they want. But usually they don't go past the reef."

"Why's that?" Joe asked.

"This place is where their food supply is," Stan said. He held out his arms and said, "Would you pass up a free meal? Besides, dolphins are totally social animals. They get lonely by themselves." Then his face grew worried. "If you're right, and Poipu's got a speargun wound, then that could be trouble."

13

The dolphin squealed under the vet's care. Dr. Cho and Maggie continued to give directions from the deck. Joe noticed that Kalea swam around Poipu, nervously squealing and whistling.

"The truth is," Stan continued, "Poipu's been getting some extracurricular exercise."

"What do you mean?" Joe asked.

Stan looked around to make sure no one was listening. Then, in a low voice, he said, "One of the scientists here, Jack Storm, takes him out for nighttime swims. Jack says the exercise keeps the dolphin's night vision at peak performance, but Dr. Cho's told him not to do it."

"Poipu must have gotten that wound during a swim last night," Joe guessed. "But where's Jack?"

"Haven't seen him," Stan said with a shrug.

Dr. Cho strode by purposefully. When she saw Stan talking to the Hardys, the head of ICS stopped short. "We need to clear this area. I'm afraid I'll have to ask you to leave," she told Frank and Joe politely. "We've got a very sick dolphin on our hands right now."

Frank cleared his throat. "Actually, I'd like to ask you something." Joe looked at his brother in surprise. Frank went on. "My brother and I are detectives, and I'm a little curious about Poipu's wound."

Cho raised her eyebrows skeptically. Joe jumped in to help his brother out. "Stan told us that a scientist here named Jack Storm takes Poipu out occasionally for night swims."

At this, Stan squirmed uncomfortably, and tried to avoid Dr. Cho's stern look.

14

"Don't blame Stan," Joe added quickly. "We were the ones asking questions. Is Jack here today?"

"Not yet," Dr. Cho confirmed. She paused a moment, holding her hand to her chin thoughtfully. "And with the dolphin being wounded, frankly I'm concerned. I plan to put in a call to him immediately."

Maggie rushed over. "Poipu's going into shock," she told Cho. "Don's got to get him into containment where he can monitor his pulse and heart rate better."

"Stan, help us out," Cho commanded. "Tell Don I'll be right there," she said to Maggie. Then the head of ICS turned to Frank and Joe. She seemed unsure of what to say to them.

"Is there anything we can do?" Frank piped up.

Cho paused for a moment, considering. "Okay, boys. Since you want to help, would you have my secretary try calling Jack? Her name is Maizie Baldwin—you'll find her desk right outside my office."

Joe thought he noticed a worried look pass over Maggie's face at the mention of Jack's name, but he couldn't be sure. "Of course," said Frank.

As soon as Cho left to attend to Poipu, Joe gave his brother a low five. "Nice going. I thought we were on vacation!" he joked. "Now you've got us working."

Frank's sandy brown hair blew in the tropical breeze. "Don't worry. We'll pass the message along to Maizie, and then we can take in some more sight-seeing." Frank paused momentarily. "That is,

15

unless Maizie can't get in touch with Jack. In which case—"

"We step in and try to find him," Joe finished for his brother.

Frank's eyes sparkled. "Exactly!"

Joe shivered, and realized that even though the sun was blazing, he was cold in his life vest and wet swimsuit. "I'll change and then we can find Maizie."

Joe and Frank headed back inside the center. Joe quickly found a men's locker room in the center's administrative wing. He changed back into his dry clothes and joined Frank in the hall. Several ICS employees strolled past, giving Frank and Joe cheerful greetings.

"I guess we look old enough to work here," Frank said with a laugh.

Like the museum and exhibition space, the administrative wing of ICS was a one-story building made out of lava rock. A long hall ran from one end of the building to the other. On one side, there were floor-to-ceiling windows that looked out on the lagoon and the coast. On the other side were cubicles and doors that led to individual offices. Open windows let in the ocean breezes.

Frank and Joe quickly found Dr. Cho's office at the end of the long hall. There, a middle-aged woman with warm brown eyes sat at a desk beside Cho's office door. A nameplate on her desk read Maizie Baldwin.

"Can I help you boys?" she asked.

When Joe told her about the accident with Poipu,

16

Maizie's eyes widened with surprise. "Dr. Cho asked us to have you call Jack at home."

Maizie quickly picked up the phone on her desk and dialed. After a moment, she hung up the phone. "No answer. It's not like Jack, not at all. I know his neighbor. I'll check with him."

With that, she dialed another number, and got through this time. From the look of concern on Maggie's face, Joe guessed the neighbor hadn't seen Jack. Maizie hung up the phone again and shook her head in confusion.

"He says he saw Jack leave late last night, but his bike is missing from his porch, and Mr. Fukuda hasn't seen him at all today."

Helen Cho walked toward them, her face set in a grim expression. "We got Poipu out of shock, but his pulse and heart rate are still dangerously low. We're just going to have to watch him carefully for the next twenty-four hours. Did you get in touch with Jack?"

"There's no sign of him," Joe reported. "He's not at home, and his neighbor hasn't seen him at all this morning."

Dr. Cho tapped her foot distractedly. "Poipu is free to swim out of the lagoon at night, so there is always a chance he might run into danger. But I know that Jack has been taking him out for swims, and I'm worried that something might have happened to the two of them. Until we find Jack, we simply won't know for sure."

"Considering what happened to Poipu, I'd suggest you call in a missing persons report on Jack," said Frank. "He could be stranded somewhere along the coast."

Cho agreed. "Maizie, you'd better call the police. Tell them to notify the coast guard, too."

"Meanwhile, why don't you let us go out and look for Jack ourselves?" Joe suggested.

At first, Cho seemed confused. Then she smiled and said, "That's right. You said you were detectives." Cho exchanged a look with Maizie, and then she raised her hands in the air. "I've got a seriously injured dolphin, a missing researcher, and two teenagers who are offering to help me out. I must be crazy. But why not? I'll get Stan to take you out in one of our speedboats. I'm sure the police will want to search the coastline as well, but you three can get started."

Fifteen minutes later, Frank and Joe were cruising out past the reef, with Stan at the helm of an ICS speedboat. On the dock, Stan had noticed that a wet suit and scuba tank were missing. So was one of the ICS motorized dinghies. It was clear to the boys that Jack had taken Poipu out for a swim. Now they hoped to find some clues as to what had happened out at sea the night before. Why had Poipu come back injured? And why hadn't Jack come back at all?

A thousand yards past the reef, Stan steered the boat south where the coastline bent around the Hardys' hotel. Joe pointed to the small, hat-shaped island he had noticed earlier.

"Devil's Hat," Stan remarked. "It's the best surfing around."

Sure enough, a dozen surfers were plowing the waves between the reef and the island. Not far away, three trawlers cruised the waters.

"Seems busy out here," Frank remarked. "You think someone on those boats might have seen Jack?"

"Hard to say," said Stan. "That one boat with the dolphin flag on its mast belongs to Jerry Finski, an ICS researcher."

Joe spotted the blue and white banner. At the prow of the ICS boat, Joe noticed a spray of water and the arc of a dolphin flying through the air. "He's got a dolphin out there with him."

"That's right, *brah*," said Stan, using one of the local expressions. "Jerry's using Maile to help lure wild dolphins to the boat."

"Cool," said Frank. "So he uses the dolphin to do research on other dolphins, right?"

"You got it," said Stan. "He could be studying the interaction between trained dolphins and wild ones."

Chugging into the waters around the northern point of Devil's Hat was an old, decrepit-looking tugboat. "Who's that?" Joe asked.

"Uncle Billy!" Stan exclaimed. "If you spend any time at all in Nai'a Bay, you're sure to meet him. He runs the scuba shop in town, but he spends most of his time looking for some old treasure."

"What kind of treasure?" Frank asked.

Stan shrugged. He steered the boat away from Devil's Hat, and north along the coast. "Who knows? Rumor has it some guy flying over Maui

19

crashed right about here. He'd stolen jewels from a bank in Honolulu and was making his getaway. His body washed ashore, and the plane was salvaged, but they never found the loot. Uncle Billy's spent the past twenty years looking for it, and he gets crazier every year he doesn't find it. At least, that's what Jack has told me. Come on, we'd better jam if we're going to do a serious search."

Stan suggested heading north, where the currents would have pulled Jack if he'd gotten caught in them. They passed Uncle Billy's beat-up tugboat and were cruising up the shore when another trawler came into view. As they sped by the fishing boat, two men aboard shook their fists at Stan.

"What's that all about?" Joe wanted to know.

"It's just the MacAllister brothers," said Stan, scowling.

"What's their problem?" Frank asked.

"ICS is trying to get Nai'a Bay recognized as a nature preserve," Stan explained. "Brad and Dan MacAllister are fishermen. The last thing they want is to have Nai'a Bay declared off-limits."

The MacAllisters had turned on their engine and were chugging toward the ICS speedboat. They stopped their boat sideways and directly in front of them, forcing Stan to cut the engine.

"Here comes trouble," Stan muttered. "How's it going, guys?"

"What're you doing out here, squirt?" the bigger of the two brothers demanded. "Nai'a Bay doesn't belong to ICS—at least not yet."

"We're looking for someone," Frank put in. "Have you seen any stranded swimmers out here?"

"Who's your friend?" the smaller brother asked, narrowing his green eyes and pushing his light brown hair out of his eyes.

"These guys are just tourists," Stan said. "Leave them alone, Dan, okay?"

Brad MacAllister shot Joe and Frank a nasty grin. "We should give these kids an island welcome, don't you think, Dan?"

"Sure," said Dan.

"I said, take it easy," Stan declared.

Brad MacAllister looped the mooring rope of their trawler onto a pinion on the ICS speedboat's deck. The two boats slid together, and Brad and Dan hopped on board the speedboat.

"Who's missing?" Dan wanted to know.

"Jack Storm," Joe told him.

"Poor Jack Storm," said Brad, crossing his arms across his barrel chest. "Good riddance, I say."

"I couldn't agree more," said Dan. "Didn't that jerk cut our nets just last week?"

"You bet he did," Brad said.

Dan leaned casually against the speedboat's railing. Frank saw Stan squirm. The ICS intern was obviously unsure of what to do next.

"I think you guys can head on back to your boat now," said Frank. "We're kind of in a hurry."

"In a hurry," said Dan.

"Kind of," Brad teased.

Joe felt the heat rise in him. Who were these two

21

punks? he wondered. From the way they talked, he wouldn't be surprised if Brad and Dan had something to do with Jack's disappearance, he decided. And from the speargun he spotted hanging on their mast, they seemed to have the means to injure Poipu.

"Listen," Joe warned. "We're not interested in trouble. But if you stay on this boat, you're trespassing, and that gives us the right—"

"To do what, exactly?" Dan asked, giving Joe a skeptical look.

"To make you leave," Joe asserted, taking a deep breath.

"Oh, really?" Brad asked. "I think we've got a tough guy here, Dan."

"I think you're right," Dan answered.

"And you know what happens to tough guys," Brad stated flatly.

"I sure do," said Dan.

With that, Brad MacAllister swung his fist around, aiming squarely at Joe Hardy's face.

# 3 Hammerhead!

Frank Hardy moved in on Brad, managing to protect Joe from the man's fist. But before Frank had a chance to take a shot at him, Brad MacAllister's leg flew out in a sharp jab. The blow hit Joe squarely in the stomach.

"Oof," Joe moaned, falling in a heap.

"Joe!" his brother cried out, racing to his aid.

Brad MacAllister stepped back. "Maybe that will give you kids the message. Maybe you'll learn what Jack Storm didn't: Stay away from Devil's Hat. Right, Dan?"

"Right," Dan MacAllister agreed.

Both brothers scrambled over the rail of the ICS speedboat before Frank, Joe, or Stan had a chance to react. A second later, Brad pulled their mooring line free, and Dan gunned the engine on their trawler. He backed their boat away, then spun it around so that it was pointing toward Devil's Hat.

"You guys are incredible," Frank called out. "We didn't do a thing to bother you."

"And now we're sure you never will," Brad called back as the boat sped away.

"Are you okay?" Frank asked his younger brother, helping him to sit up.

"I think so," said Joe, blinking several times and holding his stomach. "Who invited these guys?"

"What jerks!" Stan spat. "Those guys are the original bullies. Every time I come out here, they give me trouble. I wouldn't be surprised if they're the ones who shot Poipu and maybe even hurt Jack."

"That's exactly what I was thinking," Joe managed to say. "Did you see that speargun hanging on their mast?"

Frank nodded and helped Joe to his feet. He watched the MacAllisters sail away. "They certainly have the temperament. Maybe Jack came across them and they let their anger get the best of them."

"No 'maybe' about it," said Joe.

For the next several hours, Stan, Frank, and Joe searched the waters up and down Nai'a Bay. They sailed north all the way to Kihei, where the current changed, and then south clear down to Makena. Even after a careful check of every inlet, however, they found no sign of Jack. They even stopped at Uncle Billy's tugboat. He was as eccentric as Stan had described, suggesting that the boys were really searching for treasure, not for Jack.

24

They cruised toward the ICS trawler and Joe noticed that there were two dinghies tied to its stern. "Check it out," he told the others, nodding in the direction of the boat.

"That's odd," said Stan. "Why would Finski have *two* dinghies?"

"Maybe one is Jack's!" Joe exclaimed.

"I hope so," Stan said. He swung alongside Finski's boat.

Finski, a kind-looking man with curly black hair, looked concerned when Stan told him that Jack hadn't reported for work that day. "It's unlike him to be irresponsible," Finski said.

"ICS is missing some scuba gear and a dinghy," Frank said, "and we think Jack took Poipu out for a swim last night."

"We noticed your extra dinghy and wondered if it was his," Joe added.

Finski banged his head with the palm of his hand. "I can't believe I didn't make the connection. I guess I'm just an absentminded researcher." He gestured to the Hardys and Stan. "Sail around and meet me at the back of the boat."

Stan cruised them around to the stern of Finski's trawler. Maile frolicked in the wake of their speedboat. At the stern, Finski stood waiting. There, he hauled in a mangled dinghy that was tied up to his trawler. The inflatable tube was flat, the motor was falling off, and the dinghy only had one oar tied to it.

"I found the dinghy this morning. I was sailing around the southern shore of Devil's Hat." He drew in a sharp breath. "I figured it floated free from ICS. But if what you say is right, this must be the dinghy Jack took out last night."

Frank and Joe exchanged a worried look, while Stan let out a long whistle. "It seems as though Jack might have gotten into some serious trouble," Frank remarked. "Let's take the dinghy back to ICS."

"We should keep looking for Jack, too," Joe put in. "If he washed ashore somewhere, he could be tired, hungry, or even hurt."

The Hardys said good-bye to Finski, and Stan sailed them away from the researcher's trawler. They were starving by now, and they ate a lunch Stan had packed.

They searched until the sun started setting and the waters became dark. All three agreed they should head back to ICS.

"I don't get it," Joe said as they headed to shore. "We searched everywhere, but there wasn't any sign of Jack."

"Except the remains of his dinghy," Frank pointed out.

"We could go back out tomorrow and search around the ocean side of Devil's Hat," Stan suggested. "Maybe he swam ashore there."

"It's possible," Frank agreed. He tried not to think about the other reasons why they might not find Jack. "We've got to cover all the bases."

The setting sun cast a bright orange glow in the sky over ICS. The lagoon was peaceful and Kalea romped and played as they pulled up to the dock.

"Maybe Jack ran into the MacAllisters during his swim," Frank speculated aloud.

When they reached the dock, Stan cut the engine and tied the speedboat up to its mooring. Helen Cho came out of the ICS offices. Maggie was with her, and both women looked at the three boys expectantly.

"Any luck?" Maggie asked.

"I'm afraid not," said Frank. "But we did find this." He hauled the ruined dinghy onto the dock. "Jerry Finski found it early this morning around Devil's Hat."

At the sight of the dinghy, Maggie looked as though she was about to cry. "He's got to be out there, I just know it!" she said adamantly.

"What do you know about Jack's swims?" Dr. Cho asked Maggie.

Suddenly Maggie was quiet. "Nothing," she mumbled.

"You and Jack are friends, right?" Cho pressed. Reluctantly Maggie nodded. "So why did he persist in taking Poipu out at night, after I told him it was unsafe and I would have to let him go if he continued?" Cho asked.

Maggie dug her hands into the pockets of her shorts. "I told you, I don't know."

"I think you do," Cho said, her hands folded across her chest.

Maggie let out a frustrated breath. Frank watched the two women square off in the near darkness. Finally Maggie turned and stormed off, leaving Dr. Cho standing there, perplexed.

27

"I don't know what is wrong with that girl," Cho said. "Why won't she cooperate?"

Frank rubbed his tired eyes. "Maybe we'll get through to her tomorrow. She's upset about Jack's disappearance. Meanwhile, I'm sure Mom and Dad are worried about us," Frank told Joe. "We'd better head back to the hotel."

"Thanks for your help," Dr. Cho said as she walked the Hardys through the Center and out to the parking lot. The museum and exhibition hall were eerily quiet. Outside in the parking lot, there were only a few cars left. "The police will start an informal search tomorrow, but they won't consider Jack missing until he's gone forty-eight hours. In the meantime, I hope you two can find out what happened to Poipu—and Jack, too."

Back at the resort, Frank and Joe had dinner with their parents in the hotel's restaurant. Mr. Hardy was curious about the details of the case. When Mrs. Hardy heard about their run-in with the MacAllisters, she told her sons to be careful.

"They sound like dangerous men," she said, taking a sip of her coffee.

"You're right," Joe told her. "They're ruthless. But I'm not afraid. In fact, I think we should pay Brad and Dan a little visit tomorrow. They obviously know a lot about what's going on at Devil's Hat, and I've got some questions to ask them about Jack Storm."

"Good idea," Frank agreed. He dug into a huge piece of chocolate cake. "Let's question Uncle

Billy, too. With all his treasure hunting, he probably has a good idea of everything that's going on in the water around the island."

"You know," Joe said slowly, "I wonder if somehow this mystery is tied up with that treasure."

"All the more reason to talk to Uncle Billy," Frank said.

The Hardys stayed up for a little while watching a movie on TV in Mr. and Mrs. Hardy's room. When it was over, Frank and Joe headed across the hall to their room. Before they got into bed, Joe looked at himself in the mirror and made a series of nasty faces.

"What are you doing?" Frank asked, staring at his brother.

"Practicing." Joe smiled. "When I see those MacAllister creeps tomorrow, I want to be sure I give them the meanest look possible."

"Please," said Frank. He punched his pillow and buried his head in it. "You're going to need more than mean looks with those guys. Turn off the light and let's get some sleep."

Joe was up at six the next morning. He took one look out the hotel window and pushed his brother awake.

"Surf's up, *brah*," Joe said, imitating Stan Ho'opi'i's speech. "Let's catch a few before breakfast."

"Mmmph," Frank muttered into his pillow. "What about the MacAllisters?"

"I realize we've got a big day ahead of us," said

Joe. "But before we start investigating, I want to check out this famous Maui surf."

Joe threw on a T-shirt, shorts, and thongs. By the time he was dressed, Frank had gotten up, too. The two brothers applied sunblock, and then headed out to the beach in front of the hotel. There, the surfboard rental shack was already open. Joe picked out a couple of long boards for himself and Frank.

While Frank waxed his board, Joe took to the waves. He paddled slowly and steadily, enjoying the feel of the warm water on his hands and the early morning sun on his shoulders. Up ahead, past the reef, the surf was breaking in nice even sets. So far, he and Frank were still the only ones out.

"Hey!" Joe suddenly called out. In the distance, he spotted the familiar sight of a dolphin frolicking in the waves. Then Joe noticed the ICS speedboat nearby. Joe paddled the remaining two hundred yards between himself and the boat.

"*Howzit*?" Stan asked from onboard the speed-boat. "Catching the waves?"

"You bet," Joe said. "What are you doing out here so early?"

Stan grinned and pointed at the dolphin squealing nearby. "Kalea was feeling frisky. As soon as I showed up for work, Dr. Cho asked me to take him out."

"Cool," said Joe.

For the moment, Joe was letting his board float atop the waves. Frank was still on the beach.

"Better go for it," Stan told him, nodding to the water. "These waves aren't going to wait."

"Thanks," said Joe. "See you over at ICS. I guess Frank and I will stop by later to let Dr. Cho know what's going on with our investigation."

"No problem," said Stan. He cranked the speedboat's engine. "I'll take Kalea out. Otherwise, he'll grab all your best waves. This one's a maniac for surfing!"

Joe watched the boat sail out and saw Kalea take a few last leaps before following Stan. For the next few minutes, Joe was preoccupied with getting his sea legs. He grabbed the first wave that came along and promptly wiped out. Frank was just now paddling out from the shore. Joe held off for a few more waves and then positioned himself for the next group coming in.

"Hurry up!" Joe urged his brother, paddling into place. "This set's a winner!"

"Watch out!" came Frank's warning.

"I am watching," Joe said, his eyes on the coming waves.

The perfect wave was rolling up toward him. Joe was in just the right spot. He knelt on the board and got ready to stand.

But Frank had not been warning his brother about the waves. "It's a shark!" Frank cried.

Joe clutched his surfboard. In that split second's hesitation, it was too late to grab the break. Joe steadied himself for the inevitable wipeout. As the wave tumbled him over in a spray of foam, the last thing he saw was a telltale fin—coming right at him!

# 4 A Not-So-Warm Hawaiian Welcome

Joe Hardy tumbled up and around in the wave, then sputtered and came up for air. He felt the pull of his surfboard on his ankle where it was attached to the leash. Frantically he grabbed for the board. Even before his head was out of the water, Joe started paddling desperately for shore.

"Joe, hurry!" Frank cried out. "It's right behind you."

Joe didn't want to look, but he had to know. He darted a glance over his right shoulder. The evil-looking fin was plowing a course right for him. Suddenly Joe felt a tug on the end of his surfboard. Then he heard the awful sound of the board being ripped apart.

"Yeow!" Joe cried.

He paddled even more desperately. Joe was

about to risk a look back again to see if he'd put any distance between himself and the shark when the board flew up beneath him, tumbling Joe from its safety.

This is it, Joe thought. There's no saving me now. . . .

As Joe fell through the warm ocean waters, he felt the slippery skin of a huge fish against his back. He raised his fist, somehow remembering that you could stun a shark by punching it on the nose. But before he could swing his arm around for the blow, Joe heard a familiar squeal and whistle. He opened his eyes underwater to see the warm, friendly face of Kalea. Kalea had saved him! The shark was nowhere in sight.

Feeling a shot of relief, Joe grabbed the dolphin's dorsal fin, holding on for life. Kalea sped Joe through the currents. Joe didn't think he could hold his breath underwater much longer when Kalea finally brought them both up for air.

Joe almost laughed when he saw they were right beside the ICS speedboat. "Man, oh man, that was close," he sputtered.

Stan was there to give Joe a hand up into the boat. "No kidding," Stan said. "I was sailing back in to shore when Kalea disappeared. I guess he sensed danger. That's when I saw the hammerhead. They're dangerous, man! You're lucky Kalea saved you!"

"They're trained to rescue people?" Joe asked.

Stan tossed Kalea a fish from a bucket on the floor of the speedboat. "They use echolocation—that's a kind of sonar—to sense the presence of other large fish and mammals. He probably went to check it out and then he must have heard you call out for help."

"Pretty smart," Joe said.

By the side of the speedboat, Kalea finished off his fish in two swift bites. Then he looked up at Joe expectantly and barked for another fish. Joe reached into the bucket and tossed a fish to Kalea, who grabbed it in midair.

"I'll cruise you in," Stan said. "It looks like your brother's waiting for you to head back." He pointed to the shoreline where Frank stood, his surfboard propped by his side.

"What about the shark?" Joe asked, worried.

Stan put the boat in gear. "They've already started the hunt," he said. "See those boats out there?"

Sure enough, the bay was filling up with fishing boats and trawlers. People called to one another from the boats and gestured to the waters around where Joe had seen the shark.

"As soon as we got the sighting, these guys piled into their boats. Don't worry, we'll be safe," Stan assured him. "With all these hunters around, that shark would have to be pretty stupid to hang out."

"Will Kalea be safe?" Joe wondered, watching the frisky mammal play in the wake of the speedboat.

"Kalea will spot the shark before any of those guys," Stan said. He steered the boat for the hotel's dock. "He'll warn us."

Frank was waiting when Stan pulled the speed-boat up to a mooring. "Are you okay?" he asked.

"I'm fine," said Joe. "Kalea saved me!"

"I saw," said Frank. "That was one lucky catch. The lifeguard told me that they've had shark sight-ings, but the surfers go out anyway."

"Crazy," Stan muttered. "That's the surfer men-tality. Catch the wave, worry about the sharks afterward." He shrugged, then whistled to Kalea, who was swimming in and out of the dock's pilings. "Let's go, Kalea. Time to head home."

Kalea seemed to recognize Stan's voice. He cruised over to the boat and playfully flapped the water with his tail.

"See you guys later." Stan raised a hand in farewell and edged the boat away from the dock. "Don't forget: I'll take you out if you want to check for Jack around the other side of Devil's Hat. And stay out of the water until they catch that beast, okay?"

Joe groaned. "No problem. I never want to be that close to a shark again, no matter how great the waves look."

The Hardys headed back to their room to change and shower. Half an hour later, they were having a big breakfast of pancakes, sausage, scrambled eggs, and juice in the hotel's dining room. While they were out surfing, their parents must have gotten up and had breakfast on their own, because Mr. Hardy had left Frank a note that said they were headed to the golf course for another game.

Frank had borrowed a phone book from the front desk. Now he looked up the address of Brad and Dan MacAllister and wrote it down on a notepad. After checking the street against his map of Nai'a Bay, Frank dug into his stack of pancakes.

"It looks like they live up in the hills," he said, his mouth full.

"So it makes sense to stop by Uncle Billy's first," said Joe. He took another bite of his eggs, amazed at how hungry he was. If that shark had gotten him, he would never have had another batch of pancakes again in his life! he realized. Joe shivered at the thought. "What exactly are we going to ask him?"

"I want to know more about what's going on on the water," said Frank. "There seems to be a lot of action around Devil's Hat. Maybe Uncle Billy isn't the only one looking for the treasure."

"We should check Jack's place, too," said Joe. "There could be a clue there about what might have happened to him. We might even learn why he's been taking those swims at night with Poipu, even though Dr. Cho told him he'd get fired unless he stopped."

"Good idea." Frank searched the phone book and wrote down Jack's address.

Joe took a last sip of juice, and signaled the waiter for the check. Between the near shark attack, breakfast, and the investigation ahead of them, his adrenaline was kicking in. It felt good to be on a case!

"Ready?" Joe asked.

Frank stood up from the table. "You bet I am," he said, reflecting Joe's enthusiasm.

The Hardys left a note for their parents and then hopped into their jeep. The sun was shining, with billowy clouds hanging high in the sky, and the water was a pure blue as Frank and Joe headed into Nai'a Bay. Instead of turning left toward ICS, Frank made a right and they found themselves in the middle of town. There was a movie theater, a library, and what looked like a courthouse or city hall. The pace was slow, livened by a few tourists strolling the sidewalks. After only three blocks, the Hardys came to the edge of town. On the left stood Uncle Billy's scuba shop, with a dock of its own.

The shop's entrance was around back, on the water side. Joe led the way down the flimsy dock, after noticing all kinds of boats and jetskis, all marked Property of Uncle Billy's.

"I guess the guy rents more than just scuba equipment," he remarked to Frank.

"Let's hope the stuff is in better repair than his dock," said Frank. "Or his boat for that matter."

They were passing the tugboat Joe recognized from the day before as belonging to Uncle Billy. There was a wide rust belt around the hull where it met the waterline. Hanging from the mast was a tattered skull-and-crossbones flag. The paint on the cabin was chipping, and the deck looked as if it hadn't been cleaned in years.

"No wonder Billy's searching for the treasure," Joe said with a laugh. "He could use it."

The scuba shop itself was made out of wide planks of dark wood. It was a squat building, with an overhanging roof. The sign on the door said Closed, but Joe knocked anyway.

"Come on in!" a voice inside called out.

The place was dim, with travel posters and bumper stickers and old license plates hanging everywhere. The shelves along the wall on Joe's right were filled with scuba equipment—tanks, wet suits, regulators. Propped against the left-hand wall was an assortment of boards, for surfing, boogie-boarding, and wave-skimming. Either the place had everything you'd want for a great Hawaiian vacation, Joe decided, or it was full of junk. He couldn't decide which.

A bearded man came through a door at the back of the store. Joe instantly recognized the reddened complexion, the white hair, and the thick white beard as belonging to Uncle Billy.

"How d'ya do, boys?" Billy cried out, giving them a hearty hello.

"I'm not sure if you know us," Frank began. "We were out on the bay with Stan from ICS yesterday. We were looking for Jack Storm."

"Sure I remember you," Billy said. "In fact, I've been hoping you boys would stop by."

"You have?" asked Frank.

"Yessirree." Billy smiled and stepped toward the counter.

"Why?" Joe asked, barely containing his excitement. Maybe Uncle Billy had a lead for them!

38

Without answering, Billy reached under the counter and pulled out a speargun. "So I could show you this," he said. His expression narrowed, and the smile faded from his lips. And then, silently, the man aimed the gun right at Frank Hardy.

# 5 The Mystery Goes Off-Road

Frank slowly raised his hands into the air, his eyes locked on Uncle Billy. Joe did the same.

"Easy, easy," Frank said in a calm voice. "We'll leave right now, if that's what you want."

A wide grin spread across Billy's face and the man began to laugh. Soon he was doubled over, his hands on the counter for balance, the speargun lying harmlessly beside him.

Frank was still standing there with his hands raised. Billy must have noticed, because between guffaws he managed to say, "You can put your arms down, boys. My goodness. You two look like an antiperspirant commercial!"

One glance at Joe told Frank that his brother didn't think the joke was very funny, but Frank gave

Joe a look telling him to chill out. Both Hardys lowered their arms to their sides, while Uncle Billy wiped the tears from his eyes.

"My, my, my," the man chortled. Suddenly he composed himself and stared at Frank. "I heard through the grapevine you boys are detectives."

Joe let out a whistle. "Word sure does spread fast in this town, doesn't it?"

Billy ignored Joe's question. Fingering the speargun, he said, "Thought I'd find out how much nerve you two have, especially if you're planning to get involved in Devil's Hat. Doesn't look like you got too much guts, though. You both seemed pretty scared just now—like some bully had just stolen your favorite comic books."

"Hey, wait a minute—" Joe Hardy stepped forward toward the counter.

"Joe—" Frank warned.

Billy already had his finger on the trigger of his speargun. "I wouldn't if I were you, son."

Frank put his hand on Joe's arm. "We don't hold anything against Billy, do we, Joe?"

Involuntarily Joe's face twisted itself into one of the nasty expressions he had been practicing the night before, but he kept his cool.

"No," Joe relented. "I suppose not. Except maybe his bad sense of humor," he muttered.

Billy heard Joe's last words. Frank was expecting him to level the speargun at Joe yet again. Instead, the man burst out laughing, reached over, and gave Joe a hearty pat on the arm.

41

"I like your style," Billy said. "I take back what I said just now. You kids are all right!" Billy shoved his hand out for Frank to shake. "Billy Townsend. Pleased to meet you."

Frank couldn't keep up with the guy. First he was aiming a deadly weapon at them, and now he was shaking his hand and introducing himself. He decided not to try making sense of it all. Maybe Billy had spent too much time at sea.

"Frank Hardy," he said. "This is my brother, Joe."

"Frank, Joe, my pleasure," said Billy. "What exactly brought you kids to my place this morning?"

"You were right just now," said Frank. "We are interested in what's going on at Devil's Hat. We've heard there's buried treasure there. I guess we want to know if there's some connection between the treasure and the fact that Jack Storm is missing. What is the treasure exactly?" Frank asked.

Billy perked up, obviously happy to talk about his favorite subject. For the next five minutes, he gave Frank and Joe a history of the treasure. He talked about how it had been stolen from a jewelry store in Honolulu, how the getaway plane had crashed and the thief had washed ashore on Devil's Hat.

"They searched and searched the area, but they never found the strongbox containing the jewels," Billy concluded. "And I've been looking for it ever since."

The bell on the door rang and two customers popped their heads inside. "Are you open?" the

42

man asked. "The sign says 'Closed,' but we thought we heard voices."

"Just opening up!" Billy said, greeting them with a hearty hello. "Be with you folks in a minute. Listen, boys," he said, speaking to Frank and Joe. "Believe me, it's dangerous business, the treasure at Devil's Hat. Don't mess with it if you aren't up to the challenge." He touched the speargun a last time and then tipped them both a salute. "Stop by again sometime!"

"Sure," said Frank, pushing Joe ahead of him.

"Thanks for nothing," said Joe under his breath as they were leaving. "Do we know less now than we did before?" he asked Frank in exasperation once they were out of Uncle Billy's shop. "I sure feel like it."

Frank led the way across the street. "Actually, we know a lot."

"Such as?" Joe asked.

Frank counted off the facts. "One—the treasure consists of a box of jewels. Two—"

"Uncle Billy's a crazy man," Joe finished for his brother.

"Right," Frank agreed. He climbed into the jeep and put on his sunglasses. "It seems like Nai'a Bay brings that out in people."

"What do you mean?" Joe asked, putting on his seat belt.

"On the one hand, we've got the treasure seekers. On the other hand, we've got the MacAllisters, who want to protect their fishing rights. Right now,

Dolphin Bay is looking dangerous for more than one reason," Frank said. "Let's head on over to Brad and Dan's."

Joe sighed. "I guess it's time to head from the frying pan into the fire."

"You could sound a bit more enthusiastic," Frank joked, pulling into traffic.

"You mean I don't sound excited at the possibility of getting my head bashed in?" Joe asked. "Remind me to take my vitamins tomorrow, okay? Obviously I'm not getting enough humor in my diet!"

As they were headed out of town, Frank suddenly slowed in traffic and pulled to the side of the road. "We're missing the most important lead of all," he said, checking his map.

"What?" Joe wanted to know.

"Jack Storm!" Frank said.

Checking the map against the address he'd written down at breakfast, Frank cruised halfway through town, and then made a right, heading toward the water. He pulled the car to a stop two houses in. "That's the place," he said, pointing to a one-story bungalow.

"Obviously the police haven't sealed it off yet," said Joe.

"It hasn't been forty-eight hours yet since Jack was reported missing," Frank reminded Joe.

He got out of the jeep and headed up the walk. It, too, was made out of lava rock, Frank noticed. After reaching in his pocket for a handkerchief, Frank pulled open the screen door. He didn't want to leave any fingerprints that would ruin the Nai'a Bay Police Department's investigation.

The screen door was unlocked, and so was the wooden door behind it. "Safe town," Frank said to Joe, who was standing behind him. He pushed the door open and stepped inside.

The bungalow consisted of three small rooms: the living room with a fold-out bed, a kitchen, and a bathroom. Joe started searching a desk in the living room. Frank went into the kitchen. On the refrigerator were half a dozen photographs, including several of Maggie with a man Frank guessed must be Jack. The man had eyes that were an unusual shade of hazel, and his gaze was penetrating. Some of the other pictures had a faded brown quality that Frank knew meant they were taken years ago. In one, a baby sat on the lap of a young woman, while a man stood behind with his arm around her. In another, the same man and woman were posed, alone, in front of an old-fashioned biplane.

"Check it out!" Joe called from the living room.

"What is it?" Frank asked, leaving the kitchen.

At Jack's desk, Joe was holding a greeting card in his hands. He used a handkerchief to avoid leaving any fingerprints. Frank took the card from Joe, read it, and let out a low whistle.

" 'Jack, I know you'll find what you're looking for, and all our troubles will end,' " Frank read aloud. " 'Love, Maggie.' "

"What troubles is she talking about?" Joe wondered. "And what exactly is Jack looking for? The treasure? From that note, it looks like Maggie knows more than she's telling."

Frank placed the card back on Jack's desk. "Possibly, but we could also be reading too much into this card. Let's stop by ICS and question Maggie about it after we're done with the MacAllisters. I don't see anything else here, do you?"

Joe shook his head. "Nope. But that card seems like a good lead. Let's check out Brad and Dan, then head back to ICS."

Frank led the way out of Jack's bungalow. Soon he and Joe were back in the jeep, cruising out of Nai'a Bay and up into the hills above the town. The road got narrower and steeper the higher they went. The low-lying bushes gave way to dense tropical rain forest. On one side, the road dropped off into the steep mountainside. On the other, Frank spotted several houses on stilts, built into the hillside.

"One of those must belong to Brad and Dan," Frank guessed. He searched the mailboxes for a house number. "Yup. Fourteen sixty-one. We're looking for fourteen eighty-nine. It must be close."

"Sounds like we've got company," Joe said. "Listen."

Frank heard the whine of an engine descending the mountain in low gear. He slowed down and edged closer to the right-hand side of the road to make room for the vehicle. Up ahead, the road made a bend to the left. Just as Frank was about to enter the curve, another four-by-four came out of the curve toward them.

46

"It's Brad and Dan!" Joe announced.

Frank had already recognized the driver of the four-by-four as Dan MacAllister. He slowed the Hardys' jeep and pulled to a stop.

"Hey!" Frank shouted. "Can you guys hold up a sec?"

A short distance away from the Hardys, Dan MacAllister stopped their car. "What do you want?" Brad MacAllister called out, standing up in the passenger seat of his vehicle and holding on to the roll bar.

"We wanted to ask you some questions," Joe told him.

"Oh, really?" Dan said. "Well, we've got news for you. We're on our way to the beach and we don't have time for any of your questions."

With that, Dan MacAllister put his vehicle in gear and proceeded to drive straight toward the Hardys.

"Frank!" Joe warned. "Watch out! They're about to run us off the road."

With a resounding thud, the front bumper on the MacAllisters' four-by-four made contact with the bumper on Frank and Joe's jeep. Frank began to shift out of neutral and into first gear, but it was too late. The force of the contact from the MacAllisters' vehicle pushed the Hardys' jeep backward—and dangerously close to the edge of the mountain.

"Hold on, Joe," Frank told his brother. "We're going over!"

# 6 More Treasure Seekers

Joe Hardy felt the wheels of the jeep roll backward. The back tires slipped off the road. Frank was frantically trying to get the car into first gear and accelerate forward before they would lose all their traction and fall off the mountain.

"Whee-ha!" Dan MacAllister shouted. The glee on his face was unmistakable. The MacAllisters' vehicle was still nose to nose with the Hardys' jeep, and Dan didn't look as if he was about to let up until the Hardys were done for.

"You little . . ." Joe snarled. When they were out of this jam, Joe promised himself he was going to get revenge on these creeps. And then he had a brilliant idea.

Joe felt for the parking brake and pulled up on it—hard!

"Whoa!" Dan shouted. Since he was still accelerating, Dan's car plowed into the Hardys', which was now stationary.

"Get us out of here," Brad urged him. "Fast!"

With a squeal of tires, Dan slammed the car into reverse, backed out, and then jammed into first. He peeled down the mountain, leaving Frank and Joe barely hanging on to the road.

Joe watched them leave and then dared a look out the back of the jeep. Below, the mountain dropped off—so steeply that Joe could barely make out the bottom. One of the jeep's tires was hanging over the edge, but for the most part they were okay.

"Phew," Joe said. "That was close."

Frank managed to shove the gear shift into first. The back tires spun and then caught. With a jolt, the Hardys' jeep lurched forward—and to safety.

"Let's nail those guys," Joe shouted. "They almost killed us just now!"

"My pleasure," said Frank through gritted teeth.

The Hardys roared down the mountain. Frank stuck to a safe speed on the narrow mountain path, even though Joe urged him to go faster.

"They got too good a start," Joe moaned. "We've lost them."

"Not exactly," said Frank. "Look!"

Brad and Dan's four-by-four was barely visible at the bottom of the mountain road. With a squeal of tires, the MacAllisters turned left into Nai'a Bay. A minute later, Frank was making the same turn.

"Can you spot them?" Frank asked Joe, who was

almost standing in his seat to look over the jeep's windshield.

It was almost lunchtime and the street was crowded with midday traffic. Joe craned his neck to see through the line of stopped cars.

"There they are!" he shouted. "Over by Uncle Billy's!"

Sure enough, Brad and Dan had pulled over in front of Uncle Billy's dock. Brad was headed for the dock, casually carrying several fishing rods. Dan was nowhere in sight.

Frank was still waiting to enter a four-way stop. "They're getting away!" Joe cried.

"Not on your life," Frank assured his brother.

Joe kept his eyes on Brad, who hopped on board the MacAllisters' fishing trawler. Dan came from Uncle Billy's shop carrying scuba gear. As soon as his brother was on board, Brad unmoored the boat and pulled away from the dock.

"Hurry," Joe urged his brother.

Less than a minute later, Frank and Joe were pulling into a parking space in front of Uncle Billy's scuba shop. Joe raced from the car to see the MacAllisters' boat sputtering through the ocean in the direction of Devil's Hat Island. The brothers were still close enough to the dock to spot Joe, and Dan gave him a taunting wave as they sailed out to sea.

"Those creeps!" Joe said. "Come on, Frank. We're going after them."

"In what?" Frank asked.

Joe was already on his way to Uncle Billy's shop.

The grizzled treasure hunter was surprised to see Joe and Frank back so soon.

Billy scratched the back of his neck. "What can I do you for?"

"We want to rent a boat," said Joe.

"What kind of boat?" Billy asked.

"Anything that floats," Joe told him.

Billy got out a three-ring binder and shuffled through the pages. "Let's see here. I got a speedboat, a dinghy, and everything in between."

"Give us the speedboat," Frank said. "We're in a hurry."

"I'd have to gas her up," said Billy, raising an eyebrow. "That's extra."

"Fine," said Joe. "And let us have one of those, too," he said, pointing to a row of spearguns on the wall above Uncle Billy's head.

Frank eyed Joe skeptically. "What are you planning to do?"

"Nothing, I hope," said Joe.

He reached for his wallet and paid Uncle Billy for the rental. The man took his money and went outside to gas up the speedboat.

"Be right back," said Billy.

Joe picked up the speargun and loaded it with the spare missile Billy had brought out from under the counter. The spear snapped into place in the gun, and Joe took aim through the scope.

"Just a second," said Frank. He wrestled the gun away from Joe and stared his brother down. "We're not here to hurt anyone."

Joe felt Frank's eyes boring into him. "I know,"

he said with irritation. He knew his brother was right, though.

"So let's leave this behind," Frank said. "We're just following the MacAllisters. If we catch up to them, we'll ask them a few questions, and that will be that."

Reluctantly Joe placed the speargun back on the counter. "Okay, okay," he said. "I just hope they don't decide to come after us."

Billy returned. "Everything's set. You've got a full tank and the keys are in the boat."

"Thanks," said Joe. He edged past Billy and headed for the dock where a speedboat was waiting. Like most of Billy's rentals, the boat wasn't in the greatest shape, but at least it was floating. Joe and Frank hopped on board. Frank had stopped by the vending machines next to Uncle Billy's shop and picked up a couple of sodas, some cookies, and a few bags of chips.

"I'm glad you got some food," said Joe now. "I'm starving."

Joe started up the boat. He downshifted into reverse and backed away from the dock. After they were clear, Joe shifted again, and the boat started moving forward. While Joe steered them from the dock, Frank scanned the horizon.

"I don't see the MacAllisters," he reported.

"What's that boat out there?" Joe said, pointing to a trawler moored on the bay side of Devil's Hat.

"I think that's Finski's boat," said Frank. "I recognize the flag on its mast."

"Let's head over there and see if he's spotted Brad and Dan," Joe suggested.

They sped through the calm bay, darting between the sailboats and jetskiers. Once they were clear of the bay traffic, it would be only another ten minutes or so to the waters of Devil's Hat.

Jerry Finski gave them a wave of hello as Joe pulled the Hardys' boat up to the ICS trawler. The scientist pulled off his sunglasses and ran his hand through his curly brown hair.

"What's up?" he asked. "Looking for Jack again?"

"Not exactly," said Frank. He told Finski about their run-in with the MacAllisters. "We trailed them out here, but we lost them."

"They sailed by five minutes ago," said Finski.

"Did you see where they were headed?" Joe asked.

Finski pointed south and then hooked his hand west around Devil's Hat. "They clipped through here, headed for the ocean side of the island." He started hauling in a fishing net and spoke to Frank and Joe as he worked. "Those boys are trouble," he said, shaking his head.

"You're telling us," said Joe.

Hundreds of small, multicolored fish came up in the net as Finski pulled it in. Maile came to play by the side of the boat, obviously hoping for a snack.

"Maile never swims off?" Frank wanted to know.

"Oh, but she does," Finski explained. "That's why she's so useful."

"What do you mean?" Joe asked.

"Maile's job is to find wild schools of dolphin," Finski explained. "She has a tracking device on her flipper. When I see that Maile's been gone for several hours, I use the device to find her. Sometimes I also find wild dolphins. Sometimes I just discover her playing in some great waves. But most of the time, Maile hangs around the boat with me. She likes the company, I guess."

"Or maybe it's the meals," said Joe, listening to the dolphin squeal as Finski finished pulling in the net. "Do you feed Maile the fish you catch?"

Finski grinned. "She wishes! No, actually I throw these nets out to gather information for my research. You have to study feeding habits if you're going to learn about migration. I note population, size, that sort of thing. Sometimes I even come up with a bonus."

"Like treasure?" Joe joked.

Finski looked surprised at the question. "No," he said, seeming offended. "Like eel. That, I keep. I just love to eat eel."

Joe tried to hide his disgust, but he obviously didn't do a very good job.

"They're not bad," Finski insisted. "You should taste one sometime."

"No, thanks," said Joe. "I think I'll stick to the stuff that grows on land. Like good old-fashioned potato chips! Come on, Frank, let's see if we can track those guys around the other side of Devil's Hat."

Joe and Frank cruised away from Finski's trawler.

54

For a while Maile played in the wake of the speed-boat. After half a mile or so, however, the dolphin circled around in the water and headed back to the trawler. By now, the Hardys had jetted around to the tip of Devil's Hat. Cutting left, Joe steered clear of the shallow waters and the reef that surrounded the island. Then he straightened out the tiller and made for the ocean side of the island.

"Cut the speed a bit," Frank advised him. "I'd rather sneak up on the MacAllisters if it's possible."

Joe brought the gas down and the boat became quieter. He coasted as close to shore as he could without running the risk of hitting ground.

"Let's use these coves to protect us," Joe said, pointing to the natural inlets on the island's shore.

Like the island of Maui, Devil's Hat was also volcanic. Because it faced the sea, the island's western shore was rough, with little in the way of natural beaches. For ten minutes Joe and Frank cruised from one inlet to another, keeping an eye out for Brad and Dan.

"It's as if they disappeared," said Joe.

"Not quite," said Frank. "Check it out."

As they cruised out of an inlet into open water, Joe spotted the MacAllisters' fishing trawler. Brad was sitting in the stern, a hat covering his eyes and several fishing rods perched between his legs.

"Sneak attack," Joe whispered. "The guy's asleep. He'll never know what hit him."

"Wait a sec," Frank advised, putting his hand on Joe's arm. "Where's Dan?"

Joe shrugged. "Probably inside the boat. Come on. I don't want to lose the opportunity."

But Frank was reluctant. "There's something going on here. I don't trust these guys."

"What are we waiting for?" Joe asked.

Just then, Dan MacAllister emerged from underneath the boat, dressed in full scuba gear. That was when Joe realized the fishing rods were just a ploy.

"There's only one reason I can think of why Dan MacAllister's diving the waters out here," Joe told his brother, his eyes on Dan.

"That's exactly what I was thinking," said Frank. "It seems like Uncle Billy may have company."

Were Brad and Dan MacAllister searching for the treasure at Devil's Hat?

# 7 Bad Driving

"Even more reason to think they were the ones who shot at Poipu, and maybe got rid of Jack," Joe said, his voice low. "They want the treasure all to themselves."

"Possibly. Or maybe they really are just fishing," said Frank.

"Oh, come on, Frank," Joe said. "Fishing is one thing. Diving is another! You don't put on a wet suit and go underwater to catch fish!"

The MacAllisters' boat was no more than three hundred yards away at this point. "We'd better get out of here," said Frank. "If you're right, and they are searching for the treasure, then we've got a lot to lose if they spot us out here."

"Like our lives," Joe agreed. Quietly, with the boat on low speed, he spun them around until they were facing the other way. Then Joe pushed the throttle all the way and plowed them out of there.

But the noise from the boat called attention to their presence. Frank Hardy spotted Brad pointing at them. "Uh-oh," he said to Joe. "I think we gave ourselves away just now."

Brad MacAllister started yelling and waving his fists. Dan was pulling up their anchor. A second later, he raced to the helm of their trawler. Frank heard the sound of the boat's engine roaring alive.

"They're coming after us!" he cried.

"Don't worry," said Joe. "They can't catch us. We're in a much faster boat."

"Put on full speed," Frank shouted.

Joe pushed the throttle as far as it would go. Soon they were blasting through the water, bouncing hard as they went. Joe cut the tip of Devil's Hat pretty close, and Frank heard the ominous scraping of the ocean bottom on the hull of the boat.

"Whoops," Joe said, pulling out a bit farther from the shore. "How close are they?" Joe shouted to Frank above the roar of their boat's engine.

"We're losing them," Frank shouted back. "They can't keep up."

But just when Frank thought they were out of danger, a large projectile came whizzing past. It soared beyond the boat and skidded into the water. Frank turned to see Brad MacAllister, speargun in hand, aiming at their boat.

"They're shooting at us!" Joe cried.

"Brad's got his speargun out," Frank confirmed.

He took a look over his shoulder. Another spear came flying by. Frank ducked—just in time to miss being hit by the projectile. The weapon nicked the side of the boat and spun out in the water.

"I think they're trying to scare us," Frank said.

"They're doing a great job!" Joe answered.

Frank saw his brother check the throttle, but they both knew the answer even before Joe's hand touched the mechanism. The boat couldn't go any faster. They'd just have to hope they'd outrun the MacAllisters—and their speargun.

And then, as quickly as it started, the MacAllisters' attack ended. The Hardys had cleared the other side of Devil's Hat and were halfway across the bay when Frank noticed they were no longer being followed.

"They turned around," he said gleefully. "They're cruising back to Devil's Hat."

"Why'd they quit?" Joe asked, bringing down the throttle on their speedboat.

Frank shrugged. "I honestly think they just wanted us out of there. If they are looking for the treasure, they probably don't appreciate any spectators."

Joe snorted. "Well, they're going to have quite an audience when we tell the police to bring them in on suspicion of murder."

"There's no evidence yet that Brad and Dan even were the ones who shot Poipu," Frank reminded him. "Or that Jack's been killed. Or that Brad and Dan are responsible. Right now, all we know is that

Jack is missing, and someone shot a speargun at Poipu. We've still got a lot of investigating to do."

Now that his heartbeat had returned to normal, Frank mulled over the mystery. It seemed clear that Brad and Dan weren't just upset about losing their fishing rights. Maybe they really were looking for the treasure. They could have run into Jack and Poipu and shot at them to warn them off. Maybe that was how Poipu got his wound. The question was, why hadn't Jack turned up?

"I want to stop by police headquarters," Frank told his brother as they cruised back to Uncle Billy's dock. "We need to find out if they've discovered any sign of Jack."

"Good idea," Joe agreed. "Don't forget Maggie, too. We should swing by ICS and question her about that card she wrote to Jack."

Uncle Billy was waiting for them on the dock when Joe steered the boat toward its mooring. He gave them both a broad smile. "Have a nice sail?" he asked, catching the rope Joe threw him and attaching it to a post.

"Not exactly," Joe grumbled. "Unless you call getting shot at 'nice.'"

Surprised, Billy asked, "What happened?"

"We had a little run-in with Brad and Dan MacAllister," said Frank. "They shot their speargun at us."

Billy chortled so hard, he had to bend over. When he straightened up again, his face was bright red and he was wiping the tears from his eyes.

"Guess you got too close to their territory," Billy said. "Those boys are pretty protective."

"We've learned that," said Frank. "But of what, exactly? Their fishing rights—or something else?"

Billy shrugged. "You'll just have to ask them yourselves."

"We will," Joe told him. "That is, if we ever get close enough without risking our lives."

At the police station, Frank and Joe introduced themselves to the investigating officer, Michael Lam. The three sat in Lam's tiny ground-floor office, with its view of the bay, and discussed the case. Mike Lam was young-looking and tan, with broad shoulders that made Frank wonder if he spent his off-duty time surfing. His long brown hair was neatly combed, and he wore it in a small ponytail.

"We've done an informal search of the waters up and down the coast," Lam told them. "So far there's no sign of Jack. Tomorrow morning he'll have been missing forty-eight hours. At that point, we'll begin a full-fledged search—get the coast guard involved, that sort of thing. Since Jerry Finski found that battered dinghy, we have reason to suspect Jack ran into trouble. My guess is he's shipwrecked somewhere around Devil's Hat."

"What do you know about Brad and Dan MacAllister?" Frank asked Lam.

The young detective stretched out his legs and rested his feet on the desk. Frank noticed he was wearing thongs on his bare feet. He almost started laughing. The pace on Maui sure was different than it was back home!

"Bad boys." Lam shook his head. "I grew up with Brad and Dan. They were bullies even in elementary school."

"We think they may have something to do with Jack's disappearance," Joe told the officer. He explained their run-ins with the MacAllisters, and their suspicions that Brad and Dan might have been the ones to shoot at Poipu.

"Could be," Lam agreed. "Any other leads?"

Frank shook his head. The last thing he was going to tell Lam was that he and Joe had searched Jack's apartment. He stood up, shook Lam's hand, and headed for the door. "We'll keep in touch," Frank said. "Is it okay if we go on looking for Jack ourselves?"

"No problem," Lam agreed. "Whatever you boys can do to help, I'll appreciate."

Frank and Joe headed back to the jeep. On the way to ICS, Frank stopped at a roadside restaurant to pick up lunch. Most of the menu was fish, and Frank could tell Joe didn't seem too pleased. Finally they both settled on teriyaki burgers with rice and salad. When their meal was ready, Frank and Joe sat down at nearby picnic tables to eat.

"I've hardly seen a french fry since I left Bayport," Joe said, munching on his burger.

Frank speared a cucumber on his salad. "It sure is another world," he agreed. Above the picnic table, the palm trees swayed in the offshore breeze. The air was heavy, and smelled like flowers and sea spray. "I feel like we're a million miles away from home. Even the people act different." He laughed. "Did you see Detective Lam's thongs?"

Joe finished off his burger and wiped his mouth with a napkin. He took a sip of soda and said, "Maybe we should bring a pair back for Con Riley," he said, referring to their friend on the Bayport police force. "He should cut loose at work more often, don't you think?"

"Yeah," Frank agreed. "Let's buy him an aloha shirt, too, while we're at it!"

Ten minutes later, Frank was pulling into the parking lot at ICS. The Hardys showed the guard the IDs Maizie Baldwin had provided them the day before. Once inside the museum, Frank led the way to the ICS administrative wing. Helen Cho was in her office, but the door was closed. Maizie put her finger to her lips, indicating that Frank and Joe should be quiet. From behind the door came the sound of Cho's raised voice.

"What's going on?" Frank asked.

"Maggie Cone's getting put on probation," Maizie told them.

"Why?" Joe asked.

"She was caught trying to leave the lagoon with Kalea," Maizie explained. "Dr. Cho told all the researchers no unauthorized swims until we find out what happened to Jack."

The door to Cho's office burst open and Maggie emerged. Her eyes were red and she was sniffing. She took one look at the Hardys and pushed her way past them, without even a hello. Helen Cho appeared at her office door. She seemed upset, and the expression on her face as she watched Maggie storm down the hallway was clearly one of concern.

"Didn't take it very well, huh?" Maizie asked.

"Maggie's going through a rough time," Cho said sympathetically. "But she's only making it harder for herself by not telling the truth. She lied to me just now about not wanting to take Kalea out. Stan saw her in scuba gear at the edge of the lagoon with the dolphin, getting ready to swim out. She won't admit why she was doing it."

"You think she was going to look for Jack?" Frank guessed.

Cho pushed a stray lock of hair behind her ear. "I can only suspect." She sighed. "Why don't you boys come inside?"

Once they were sitting down in Dr. Cho's airy office, surrounded by large, color posters of dolphins, Frank gave the director an update on where they stood. He explained to Dr. Cho that they wanted to search the waters around Devil's Hat. Frank made arrangements with Dr. Cho to have Stan take them out later. "Come by after six, when the center closes," Cho told them, seeing Frank and Joe to the door. "I'll set you up with everything you need."

Jerry Finski was coming down the hall as Frank and Joe were leaving. The researcher stopped at Cho's office. Dr. Cho said hello to him and then asked Frank, "What's your next step?"

Frank thought for a moment. "To me, the key

here still seems to be the treasure. How can we find out more about it?"

"The public library should have information on it," Cho told them. "Don't you think, Jerry?" She turned to the scientist.

"Why, yes, I suppose so," said Finski. "You can't miss it."

"Good idea," said Joe. "Thanks. Hey, wait a minute," he added. "Shouldn't you be out fishing for eels or something?"

Finski laughed. "Even the hardiest researcher has to come back to shore for supplies," the man said. "I came in on that dinghy I keep tied up to the trawler. Maile's minding the store."

Frank and Joe said good-bye to Finski and Cho. After stopping by the lagoon to make arrangements with Stan and watch Kalea play, the Hardys headed back out to the parking lot. As they were leaving, Frank noticed Maggie talking to another researcher and watching the Hardys at the same time. The minute she spotted the Hardys, Maggie went back inside the center. Frank decided to follow her. "I'll be back," he told Joe.

Once Frank got inside, he called out to Maggie, who was disappearing down the hall. "Can I ask you a few questions?" he said.

Maggie turned to Frank. She had her hands stuffed into her jeans and her shoulders were hunched. Slowly she approached him. "What's up?"

"Why did you lie to Dr. Cho about taking Kalea out?" he asked.

"I didn't lie!" Maggie replied defensively.

"Dr. Cho thinks you did," Frank responded. "And I think you were going to look for Jack." Frank thought he saw a guilty look pass over Maggie's face. "It would make sense that you would want to find him," said Frank. "He's your friend."

"Yes, he is," Maggie agreed. "But I know he'll turn up."

"Was Jack in some kind of trouble?" Frank pressed.

Maggie backed away a bit. "Why do you ask?"

"I was just wondering," said Frank. He examined his fingernails and watched Maggie out of the corner of his eye.

The young researcher's eyes darted left and right. Then she stuck out her jaw and said, "I've got to get back to work. Sorry."

With that, Maggie took off toward the administration offices. Frank rejoined Joe outside, and reported to his brother what Maggie had—and hadn't—said.

"What's she hiding?" Joe wondered aloud as they climbed into their jeep. "Why did she lie about trying to take Kalea out?" He negotiated the turn out of the parking lot. "I'm not saying she's a suspect, but my guess is that Maggie definitely knows more than she's telling."

Joe drove from the ICS complex into town. After about a mile or so, theirs was the only vehicle on the road. On either side were tall banks of sugarcane. Behind, Frank heard the telltale whine of a motorcycle engine. A mile later, the bike was still there.

When they pulled into town, the bike hung back a ways, then made a left turn and disappeared. Joe parked a half mile up, in front of the library. Frank dismissed the motorcycle, his mind already on the treasure and the research ahead of them.

As soon as they asked the librarian about the treasure at Devil's Hat, the man smiled and took them directly to a set of shelves at the back of the high-ceilinged room.

"The information on the Hawaii Heist is very complete," the man said. "Please write your name on this sign-in sheet. Because it is a special collection, you may only use the materials in the library. You can't take them out."

The librarian left. Frank went to write his name on the collection's sign-in sheet and immediately let out a low whistle.

"What is it?" Joe asked, his voice low.

"Guess who was the last person to read this stuff," Frank asked.

"I give up. Who?" Joe returned.

"Maggie Cone!" Frank whispered loudly.

For the next hour, Frank and Joe pored through the information in the file. The whole time, Frank kept his eyes peeled for some clue as to what Maggie was hoping to find among the clippings and photographs about the treasure. They learned the name of the pilot—Hank Mobley—and that the treasure was a strongbox containing several priceless pieces of jewelry.

"I can't believe no one ever found that box," said Joe, reading from an article in a yellowed newspaper. "There was a search crew out there for months. The jeweler's insurance company put up a reward, too. Whoever finds those jewels stands to earn a cool hundred thousand."

Frank was putting the documents, photographs, and articles back into the file folder from which they'd come. The whole time, he'd been thinking so much about what Maggie was looking for, he'd almost missed the most important clue of all. One of the news articles had a photograph of Hank Mobley. Looking at the photograph more closely, Frank exclaimed, "It's him! It's got to be."

"Who?" Joe wanted to know.

"The guy in the picture on Jack's refrigerator! Hank Mobley! Why would Jack have a picture of Mobley tacked to his fridge?" Frank wondered aloud. "We have to head over to Jack's to make sure. But first, I want to make a photocopy of this picture."

Studying the face in the photograph, Frank became certain it was the same man he'd seen pictured in the snapshots on Jack's refrigerator. The cleft in the guy's chin was unmistakable; so was the curly, blond hair. The question was: Where did Jack get a picture of the Hawaii Heist thief, and why did he have it on such prominent display?

Frank and Joe were both excited as they left the library. They'd finally come up with a solid clue. Joe went in search of a soda down the street, while Frank stood on the library steps, taking a deep breath of the sweet island air. Frank spotted his brother returning with two bottles of soda. Just as

Joe was crossing the street in front of the library, a motorcycle came roaring down the block.

"Joe," Frank called out. "Watch out!"

Joe stopped short in the middle of the street. The driver must not have seen him, because the motorcycle wasn't slowing down. And then Frank remembered the bike tailing them from ICS.

"Joe!" he cried. "Get out of the way! Hurry!"

But it was too late. The motorcycle rider was closing in on Joe. His brother was going to get hit, and there was nothing Frank could do about it!

# 8 The Ride of Frank's Life

Joe Hardy found himself facing the motorcycle rider. The bike was bearing down on him, and the rider wasn't about to stop.

There weren't any cars between Joe and the bike, but the few pedestrians who were crossing the street ran from the rider's path. Joe tried to move, but he felt as if his feet were frozen. He couldn't believe the guy would run him down in broad daylight, just like this!

"Joe!" came Frank's voice. *"Run."*

At the last possible second, Joe threw himself out of the rider's path. The sodas he was carrying flew from his hands and he fell to the ground. He rolled several times, protecting his head with his arms. A split second later, the motorcycle roared by—

70

inches away from Joe's head. He saw a blur of purple—the bike's gas tank—but that was all.

Joe pulled himself up and watched the motorcycle disappear down the street. Frank Hardy raced over to his brother and helped him to his feet.

"Who was that creep?" Joe said, trying to catch his breath.

"I didn't get a good look at him," Frank said. "Did you see anything?"

Joe shook his head. "Not with the helmet and goggles he was wearing."

"Come on," said Frank. He headed across the street toward their car. "We're not letting him get away, that's for sure."

There was only one road from Nai'a Bay to the main highway. Joe said he had seen their motorcycle man turn left from the main street onto that road, so Frank headed in its direction. When the Hardys got to the highway, they looked right and left. There was no sign of the rider. Frank drove a short way in both directions, but their suspect was gone.

"He couldn't have just disappeared into thin air," said Joe.

Frank pointed out the dirt roads that turned out every two hundred yards or so into the fields of sugarcane. "He could have taken any one of these paths," Frank told him.

Joe pounded his fist on his thigh. "What'll you bet it was one of the MacAllisters?"

"I doubt it," said Frank.

"Why?" Joe asked.

"Because whoever it was followed us from ICS." Frank quickly explained about seeing the motorcycle behind them on the way into town. "Did you notice Brad or Dan hanging around the dolphin center?"

Joe made a face. "Not exactly." Then he had an idea. "Let's report the incident to Mike Lam. He might be able to trace the bike."

Ten minutes later, the Hardys were back at the Nai'a Bay Police Department. Lam wasn't in, but Joe gave a full report on the incident to the officer on duty. Although he couldn't remember the license plate, Joe was able to give a description of the bike—that it was purple with chrome trim. The man promised to have Lam call them at their hotel if he had any leads.

"Where to now?" Joe asked his brother as they stood outside police headquarters. A light rain began to fall, even though the sun was still shining.

Frank checked his watch. "It's only four-thirty. We're not due at ICS until six. Let's stop by Jack's apartment and check out those photographs. We need to compare the picture of Hank Mobley to the one on Jack's fridge."

"Cool," said Joe. "Can we stop and pick up a soda on the way? That motorcycle rider pretty much ruined those other pops."

After grabbing a couple of soft drinks, Frank and Joe headed over to Jack Storm's place. The police still hadn't sealed the bungalow. The Hardys went in the way they had earlier in the day. Frank headed straight for the kitchen. Joe was right behind him. When Frank pulled two photographs from the refrigerator, Joe watched over Frank's shoulder as his brother compared the two photographs to the copy he'd made at the library.

"It's him," said Frank. "I knew I recognized the photograph."

Sure enough, the man in the pictures from Frank's fridge was none other than Hank Mobley, the Hawaii Heist thief! He had the same curly blond hair, the same cleft in his chin.

"But what's Jack doing with a picture of Mobley?" Joe wanted to know.

"That's what we have to find out," Frank told him. "I think we need to search this place once more to see what else we find."

Joe nodded in agreement. "I'll take the bedroom. You can have the living room."

While Joe searched the bedroom, Frank took on Jack's cluttered desk. Not five minutes later, Joe heard his brother call out his name. "Joe! I think I've got something."

Joe went into the living room to find his brother standing at Jack's desk. Frank had removed a section of the desk from the back, and was standing next to it with a piece of paper in his hands.

"A secret compartment, huh?" Joe asked. "So Jack has something to hide?"

"You bet he does," said Frank. He handed the sheet of paper to his brother. Joe took out a handkerchief and used it to hold the paper.

"This looks like a map of Nai'a Bay," said Joe.

"That's exactly what it is," Frank agreed.

"But what are all these *X*'s?" On the map, the waters of Nai'a Bay were divided into even blocks. The blocks were numbered. The first twelve spots —the waters closest to the town of Nai'a Bay— each had a large *X* drawn through it. A chart on the back of the map listed the numbered blocks, with dates beside the first twelve that corresponded to the blocks that were crossed out on the map. The first date was from six months earlier, and the most recent one was from only a week earlier. Checking the map again, Joe noticed that the next numbered block was a spot in the waters directly in front of Devil's Hat.

"Unless I'm wrong, Jack Storm's been searching these waters," Frank said. "That map is pretty systematic. It looks like Jack's spent the past six months searching these spots, one by one. If he followed this map as closely as it seems, he must have been about to search the waters on the bay side of Devil's Hat when he disappeared."

Joe felt his excitement rising. "This means Jack was definitely looking for the treasure," he said.

"It seems that way," said Frank.

"And he ran into someone else looking for the treasure, and that person shot at him or Poipu or both," Joe concluded in a rush.

Frank held up his hand to slow his brother down. "Wait just a minute," said Frank. "We don't know any of that. There're still too many unknowns."

"Such as?" Joe asked.

74

"Why did Jack have Poipu out with him? Does this map prove he was looking for the treasure? If so, did anyone else know about Jack's search?" Frank paused. "Should I go on?"

Joe leaned against Jack's desk and studied the map. "No, thanks," he told his brother. "I get the point."

Without saying a word, Frank strolled out of the room. "Where are you going?" Joe called after him.

A moment later, Frank returned with a coffee mug in his hand. "What are you doing?" Joe asked.

"What we should have done in the first place," said Frank. He wrapped the mug in his handkerchief. "Get a set of Jack's prints and fax them to Con Riley. I want to know as much as we can about this guy: where he comes from—"

"If he's got a record," Joe put in.

"Precisely," said Frank.

"I'm glad I thought to bring our fingerprinting kit," Joe said to his brother.

Frank laughed and gave Joe a shove on the back. In Bayport, when Joe put their full detective kit into his duffel, Frank had given him a hard time. "'You never know when you'll run into a mystery,'" Frank now quoted Joe.

"And you should always be prepared," Joe finished for him now.

For the next hour, Frank and Joe rushed through their tasks. The coffee cup gave them a nice set of prints, and they got it back to Jack's apartment with ten minutes to spare. At six exactly they were pulling into the ICS parking lot. The guard was just locking up the doors to the museum. Frank and Joe showed him their IDs and he let them through.

"I just thought of something," Joe said as they headed back toward the lagoon. "Remember that card Maggie sent Jack?"

"'I hope you find what you're looking for,'" Frank quoted. "The treasure! That confirms it!"

Joe beamed at his brother. Another piece of the mystery had fallen into place. Then his expression grew serious. "Maggie really does know more than she claims. We should talk to Dr. Cho about this lead as soon as possible."

Stan was at the lagoon, putting Kalea through his paces. He gave the Hardys a wave of hello and said, "Want to learn some rudimentary dolphin training techniques?"

"Sure," said Joe. He went to stand beside Stan, who wore thongs, a blue ICS T-shirt, and white swim trunks. Obviously, getting wet was part of the job, because every time Kalea came jumping out of the water, he splashed Stan with a spray of water. The ICS intern was already pretty wet. Joe was grateful for the T-shirt and shorts he wore.

"I'm having Kalea find his hoop underwater," Stan explained. The dolphin came up with the hoop in its mouth, leapt into the air, and gave it to Stan, who held his arm aloft. "Some of the dolphins here are trained with hand signals, others use sound commands. Poipu is trained with a combination of hand signals and video images."

"Where's the video?" Joe asked.

76

Stan pointed to a camera set up by the side of the lagoon. "The monitor is underwater. See down there?"

Joe bent to look underwater at the wall of the lagoon. Vaguely he could make out a TV monitor set into the wall. "This is all pretty advanced," Joe said, standing up again. "Which commands are working best with the dolphins?" he asked.

Dr. Cho had come over while Stan was talking. Frank was with her. Now Cho spoke up. "That's a good question," she said with a smile. "It depends on who you ask."

The ICS director took Kalea's hoop from Stan. She went to the side of the lagoon, tossed the hoop underwater, and made a series of hand gestures. First she put her hand to her forehead, as if she were making a salute. Then she made a fist and traced a big circle in the air. Finally she held out both her hands toward Kalea.

"Dr. Cho just told Kalea to find his hoop," Stan explained. "The saluting gesture means 'find.' The circle she made is the signal for 'hoop.' Finally, she pointed at Kalea as if to say 'you.'"

Kalea began circling the lagoon, whistling and squealing as he went. Thirty seconds later, he emerged, the hoop in his mouth. Without any further instructions, he swam over to Dr. Cho, leapt into the air, and deposited the hoop in her hand.

"Cool!" Frank cried out. "It looks like he's having a blast."

"He is," Joe agreed. "You should try swimming with him."

"You mean your brother hasn't been in the lagoon with the dolphins?" Cho asked, surprised.

Frank shook his head. "No," he said.

"Get this man a life vest and a pair of swimming trunks!" Cho insisted. "You can't pass up an opportunity to swim with dolphins. It's a once-in-a-lifetime event!"

Frank was thrilled. Now he'd have his chance to go for a swim with these amazing creatures. The group laughed when he grabbed Stan's arm and practically dragged him into the locker room. Five minutes later he emerged, wearing trunks and a life vest, ready for his swim. While Joe gave his older brother encouragement, Frank got into the lagoon.

"Just let him swim between your legs," Joe offered.

"Listen to the pro," Stan joked. "Already giving advice!"

In the water, Frank Hardy at first felt excited. But he was soon disappointed. Kalea circled him once, then seemed to be distracted. Clicking and squealing, the dolphin shot off toward the reef.

"I guess he didn't like your looks!" Joe shouted out. He and Stan burst out laughing. Even Dr. Cho was trying to hide a smile.

Frank grinned ruefully and swam back to shore.

Stan gave him a hand out of the water. "Don't feel bad, *brah*," he said. "Kalea just found someone more his type to play with."

Frank looked out across the water. There were two dolphins now. One was making a beeline for ICS, while Kalea frolicked in the wake.

"That dolphin seems to be in some kind of hurry," Frank commented.

Dr. Cho squinted, trying to see in the bright sunlight. "If I'm not mistaken, that's Maile."

"Something must be wrong," said Stan. "Maile's been trained not to leave Dr. Finski's boat except to find wild dolphins."

"What reason could she have for heading in to shore?" Frank asked.

"I think I know," said Dr. Cho. She was leaning over the side of the lagoon with Maile's rostrum in her hand. The dolphin's mouth was open. Dr. Cho reached her hand inside. "She must have wanted to show us this."

Dr. Cho held up a man's stainless steel diving watch. "Want to take a look?"

Frank took the watch from Dr. Cho's outstretched hand. Joe peered over his shoulder. On the back he read the engraving: " 'To J.S. From M.C.' " He and Joe exchanged a look.

"J.S. means Jack Storm. This watch belongs to Jack Storm!" Frank announced.

# 9 Sniper Fire!

For a moment the group looked at each other in shocked silence. "Could that mean he's still alive?" Stan cried.

"Maybe," said Frank. "But it could also mean that Jack is dead, or that the dolphin simply found this watch somewhere and Jack is long gone."

"I'm with Stan," Joe said optimistically. "I think Maile found Jack, and he sent his watch back so that we'd bring help."

Frank handed the watch back to Dr. Cho and then turned to watch the dolphins frolic in the lagoon. "If only they could talk—we could ask them," he said.

Dr. Cho agreed. "Unfortunately, we're only at the point where we can talk to them, and not vice versa. We're miles away from understanding their communication, which simply proves how great their intelligence is. They can understand us, but we can't understand them!"

"I just know it means Jack is alive," Stan insisted. "And that he's in danger! Otherwise, he'd come back on his own."

"Let's hope we see some sign of him when we go out," Joe put in. "If he is alive, we're bound to find him at some point."

"Which reminds me," said Stan. "I tried getting the speedboat started before you got here. It's not working right. The thing stalls as soon as I put it in gear."

"Can't we rent one from Uncle Billy?" Joe asked.

Stan's face lit up. "That's a great idea. His shop's probably closed by now, but we can call him at home and set it up. He lives right next door to the shop. It shouldn't be a problem."

"So that's settled. Meanwhile, I'd better put in a call to Jerry on his ship-to-shore phone," said Cho. "He must be worried about Maile."

Frank remembered the set of prints he had with him. "Since you're going back there," he said to Dr. Cho, "can we ask you a favor? Can we use your fax machine to send something to a friend of ours back home in Bayport?"

"No problem," said Cho. "It sounds important."

"It is," said Frank. He knew now was the time to share his suspicions about Jack with Dr. Cho. It wouldn't be a pleasant conversation, but he had to let the director know the track he and Joe were on.

While Stan and Joe went to call Uncle Billy,

Frank went with Dr. Cho to her office. The director switched on the lights and the fax machine, and then put in a quick call to Finski. From the part of the conversation Frank overheard, he could tell the researcher had been worried about Maile and was relieved to know the dolphin was okay.

"Jerry's coming in tomorrow to pick her up," Dr. Cho said when she was off the phone. "He said he was about to use his tracking system to locate Maile when I called."

Frank pulled out the sheet of fingerprints he'd taken from Jack's coffee mug. "Here's what I want to fax," he told Dr. Cho.

Cho took the paper from him and dialed the number Frank had written down. "You want to tell me who these belong to?" she looked up to ask as the paper went through the fax machine.

"Actually, they're Jack's." At Cho's surprised expression, Frank explained what he and Joe had uncovered so far. "We have reason to think that Jack knew Hank Mobley, the Hawaii Heist thief. We also believe he may have been searching for the treasure at Devil's Hat."

Helen Cho's eyes immediately clouded over with worry. "Jack Storm was my best researcher. *Is,*" she corrected. "You should be careful what you say."

"I realize that," said Frank. "Still, we have to consider the possibility that Jack was using Poipu and his nighttime swims as a decoy while actually searching for the treasure."

"I'd be very surprised to learn that Jack cared

more about some sunken treasure than his own dolphin," Cho insisted.

"It's only a theory right now," said Frank.

Dr. Cho rested her elbows on her desk and leaned forward. "If so, was Maggie involved?"

Frank smiled at Dr. Cho's sharp instincts. Nothing got past the woman. "That's also a possibility," he confirmed. "We can't rule it out."

Cho shook her head sadly. "Then I really will have to keep an eye on Maggie. One more false step from her, and she won't just be on probation. She'll be fired!"

The fax machine beeped to signal that it was sending Jack's prints through. "I thought I was such a good judge of character," Cho said, shaking her head sadly. "And now I come to find out that one of my star researchers might very well be nothing more than a treasure seeker—with a record!"

Frank tried to reassure the woman. "Maybe we're wrong. We simply have to cover every base."

Stan and Joe were waiting for Frank when he emerged from Cho's office. Joe had packed a duffel with a flashlight and a first aid kit. "Just in case we stay out past dark," Joe said.

"Some cover might not be bad," Frank pointed out. "We might find ourselves with the chance to spy on a treasure seeker or two."

Stan's eyes gleamed with excitement. "Let's hope so, *brah*."

After packing some food in case they were out late, and calling their parents to let them know where they were, the Hardys and Stan headed over to Uncle Billy's. The man was making some final checks on a speedboat at the dock.

"You boys aren't planning to do some treasure hunting, are ya?" Uncle Billy asked.

"Maybe, maybe not," Stan told him, hopping aboard the speedboat. "Wouldn't you like to know!"

Billy guffawed. "Everything's set," he told the Hardys. "Have a pleasant trip."

Under Stan's guidance, they steered out of Nai'a Bay and toward Devil's Hat. After a ten-minute cruise, they were trolling the waters around the infamous island. They spotted Finski's trawler and swung by to assure him that Maile was okay. Then Stan made the slow tour of all the inlets on the bay side of Devil's Hat, while Frank and Joe kept their eyes peeled for some sign of Jack. If they spotted any kind of movement onshore, they planned to bring the boat closer in and then swim the rest of the way.

Two hours later, Stan and the Hardys had covered the entire bay side of Devil's Hat, and half of the ocean side, too. They hadn't seen anything on the island or in the waters surrounding it. They trolled so slowly, Frank thought they could walk faster, but he knew they were just being thorough. The only way to find Jack was by searching carefully and slowly.

Around eight o'clock, the sun started to set in a wild display of orange and red. Stan anchored the boat, and the boys ate their dinner of tuna fish sandwiches and macaroni salad. Frank kept his eyes focused on the darkening shadows that covered Devil's Hat. But nothing moved in the dusk light, and nothing stirred on the island's volcanic slopes.

"We'll have to go in soon," Joe remarked.

Stan started up the boat again. He cruised them toward the northwestern point of the island. "From here, we've only got the northern tip to search, and then it's back to the bay side. Let's stay out a little while longer and finish our search."

"Sounds like a good plan," Frank agreed.

Just as they were rounding the tip of the island, Frank spotted a trawler a short distance away. It was the first sign of life—besides Finski's boat— that they'd seen the whole evening. The question was: Who was in the trawler, and what were they doing out at Devil's Hat at night?

"Company," Joe murmured beside Frank, his eyes on the trawler. "Do you recognize the boat?"

Frank shook his head. There were no markings on the boat—no flag, and no name that he could read on the bow. Slowly the trawler moved north, into the path of their speedboat.

"What's up with that *lolo*head?" Stan asked, cutting the throttle on their boat. "He's headed into our path. Is he nuts?"

"If it's the MacAllisters," Joe said, "I've seen them do crazier things."

The trawler chugged closer. By now it was headed on a course straight for the speedboat. Even by cutting the power on their boat and taking a sharp turn right, Stan would have trouble avoiding a collision.

"I gotta get us clear!" Stan shouted.

Putting on a burst of speed, he cut their boat even harder to the right. The Hardys' boat spun sideways in the water, coasting parallel to the trawler.

Even though they were still at least a hundred feet from the boat, Frank trained his flashlight beam on the trawler to see if he could figure out who was at the helm. Just as his light came on, a shot rang out. Frank heard a bullet whiz by the speedboat's bow. He was trying to make sense of what was going on when he heard another shot.

Frank ducked. "They're shooting at us!" he cried out to Stan. "Get out of here, fast."

# 10 Some Highly Suspicious Training

As soon as Joe heard the shots, he hit the deck. Next to him, Stan crouched down and gunned the gas on the speedboat. Out in the water, the gunshots stopped. Joe detected the sound of the trawler sailing off.

"It's getting away!" Joe cried, kneeling to have a better look. Sure enough, the trawler was sputtering out to sea, and had already gone a good hundred yards. "We can't let that happen. We've got to find out who that was."

"And get shot at again?" Frank demanded. "I don't think so!"

"We'll take evasive action," Joe shot back. "Help me out here, Stan."

Stan Ho'opi'i shrugged his broad shoulders. "I'm up for the chase if you are."

"Let's do it!" Joe cried. He stood up and took the throttle from Stan. "I'll drive."

But five seconds after Joe pushed the boat to top speed, he felt them losing ground. The trawler chugged off to sea, into the darkness, while the speedboat sputtered, gave a last gasp, and died.

"What's wrong?" Frank wanted to know.

Joe flipped the ignition several times, but the boat wouldn't respond. "We're out of gas!" He slammed his fist against the instrument panel and noticed that according to the gas gauge, they still had half a tank. "The gauge must be busted. Or else there's something else wrong with the boat. Whatever it is, this tin can doesn't want to go."

"Maybe all that shooting scared it," Stan joked.

Frank made an effort to resuscitate the boat, but nothing seemed to work. "We're going to have to radio in for help," he said. "I hope Uncle Billy sticks close to his CB."

It took them almost half an hour, but they were finally able to get through to Uncle Billy on the radio. The scuba shop owner promised to head on out to rescue them. While they waited for him to show up, Joe became convinced that it was all Billy's fault they had run out of gas.

"He doesn't want us out here investigating," Joe insisted, keeping his eyes peeled in the darkness for Billy. "He purposely half filled the tank so we'd get stranded."

"If that's true," Frank pointed out, "why does the gas gauge still read half-full?"

"And why'd he give us enough gas to sail all the way around Devil's Hat?" Stan put in.

Joe glared at them both, realizing they each had a point. "I don't know," he grumbled. "I just don't trust the guy."

"If you want something to mull over, think about the shooting," Frank told his brother. "Did you recognize that trawler?"

Joe frowned. "It was too dark. My guess is that it was the MacAllisters'."

The three boys sat in silence for a while. After about fifteen minutes, Joe heard the sound of a boat sputtering toward them. Out of the darkness, a fishing trawler appeared. For a split second, Joe almost ducked. What if it was the MacAllisters coming back for a second round?

But Uncle Billy's grizzled face appeared in the beam of Frank's waning flashlight. "I had to borrow this boat from one of my customers in the marina," Billy called out to them. "I couldn't get that little tugboat of mine to start."

Uncle Billy handed over a red container. "There's your gas," he told them. "I'll wait and follow you boys back to shore."

As Stan and Frank filled the boat's tank with gas, Joe thought about the possibility that Uncle Billy had been the one to shoot at them. The MacAllisters were prime suspects, sure, but Billy could have been out trolling the waters earlier in his borrowed trawler. In fact, what if he borrowed the fishing boat just to make it seem as if Brad and Dan were the ones shooting at them? He could have gotten the Hardys' SOS on the radio inside the trawler, and simply cruised back just now.

Stan got the boat started. He aimed them back to shore, and Uncle Billy followed in their wake. While they were cruising, Joe shared his suspicions with his older brother. Frank scowled skeptically.

"Billy hasn't been a suspect up until now," Frank reminded him. "Aren't we still going on the assumption that the MacAllisters are looking for the treasure, too, and that they would do anything to stop someone else from finding it?"

"I guess," Joe admitted. In the darkness he stared behind them and watched Uncle Billy. "But the guy's got a big stake in the treasure. *And* he's crazy enough to come out here and shoot at us—just to give us a little scare. He did it before with that speargun."

Frank seemed to consider Joe's theory. "You could be right." Then Joe saw him frown. "This case is so frustrating. Until we find Jack, all we have to go on are assumptions."

"Then let's hope we find Jack," said Joe, "and soon."

The next morning, Frank got up early. He put in calls to Helen Cho and Mike Lam, only to learn that neither was in yet. Joe slept late, obviously exhausted from the night before. By the time they had gotten back to Uncle Billy's and dropped Stan off at his apartment, then gotten back to their hotel, it was nearly midnight. Then Frank and Joe spent another half hour talking to their dad about the case. Fenton Hardy agreed that their leads were still pretty inconclusive, but he urged his sons to be patient. They were sure to get a break soon.

Now Frank nudged Joe awake. "Come on, sleepyhead—we're supposed to meet Mom and Dad for breakfast in ten minutes."

With a groan, Joe sat up, rubbed his eyes, and mumbled, "Go ahead. I can't wake up that quickly."

"Yesterday morning you were up at six, ready to catch the waves," Frank reminded him.

"That was yesterday." Joe fell back against his pillows and pulled the blanket over his head. "Today is a different story."

Frank went down to find his parents in the hotel's main dining room. Mr. and Mrs. Hardy were already sipping their coffee when Frank arrived.

"You sure you don't want to come with us to see the volcano this morning?" Mr. Hardy asked Frank. "It's supposed to be pretty exciting."

Frank was torn. Because of their case, he and Joe were missing some great sight-seeing. But he had to say no. "I think we're going to crack this one soon," he told his father. "As soon as we do, Joe and I will have time for that."

"But until then, you're too preoccupied to enjoy the sights anyway," Mrs. Hardy said, smiling.

"I guess so," Frank said ruefully.

Joe arrived and the Hardys enjoyed a pleasant breakfast. Joe had his favorite—french toast—and Frank ordered a pancake sandwich. The whole time he ate, though, Frank kept itching to get up and call Cho again. Con Riley might have already gotten information on Jack's prints and been able to fax a reply back to ICS. Then there was Mike Lam— maybe he'd have information for them about who owned the motorcycle that tried to run down Joe.

"Earth to Frank," came Joe's voice. "Calling Frank Hardy. Come in, Frank."

Frank looked up to see his parents standing beside the table with Joe by their side.

"Are you ready to get started, or do you want to sit here and daydream all morning?" Joe asked.

"You're the one who slept in," Frank grumbled.

"Doesn't look like either of them got up on the right side of the bed, does it?" Mrs. Hardy asked her husband.

Frank's father shook his head. "I don't know what's wrong with these kids—I'm going to enjoy my vacation!"

"See you," Laura said, giving both Frank and Joe a kiss. "Leave a message about whether or not you'll be here for dinner."

Frank and Joe walked out with their parents. Mr. and Mrs. Hardy got into their rented sedan, while Frank hopped into the passenger seat of their jeep. "You can drive," he told Joe.

"Thanks, *brah*," said Joe, putting on his shades and starting up the car. "Where to?"

"ICS first," Frank told him. "After we check the fax machine, we can call Mike Lam to see if he's got any news for us about that motorcycle."

It was another glorious day, with the trade winds

92

blowing offshore, the sky a clear blue, and the smell of flowers in the air. The slopes of the West Maui Mountains were a deep green. Frank thought of his parents, hiking the volcano to the top. He hoped he and Joe would get to do some sight-seeing before they all left in a few days.

When they pulled into the parking lot at ICS ten minutes later, Joe said to Frank, "I don't think we need to visit Mike Lam after all. Check this out."

In the parking lot were two other vehicles. One was an old VW bug. The other was a motorcycle—purple with chrome trim—just like the one belonging to the rider who had nearly run down Joe the day before.

"Break number one," Frank muttered. "Maybe this'll be our lucky day after all."

"So our motorcycle rider works at ICS," Joe said, parking the car. "I give you three guesses who it might be."

"No problem," said Frank. "Maggie Cone. She's the only person I can think of who works at ICS and also might want us off the case."

"She certainly hasn't been very cooperative," Joe agreed. "But don't forget that a friend of hers might have borrowed the bike. Or that there might be others in town like it. Come on, let's head inside and see what we can find out."

Although the museum wasn't open yet, a guard at the door let Frank and Joe inside. Frank led the way through the museum to the administration offices. A quick look told him that the hallway was dark and that the office at the end—Dr. Cho's—was empty.

"She's still not in yet," Frank said.

"But look who is," Joe said, pointing out the glass windows that faced the lagoon. There, Maggie Cone was dressed in a scuba suit, putting Kalea through some paces. Stan was there, too, straightening the area around the lagoon and watching Maggie train Kalea.

"That girl's got some serious questions to answer," Frank said. "We're not letting her off this time."

As they walked out to the area around the lagoon, Stan gave both Hardys a wave of hello. He had a hose and was busy watering down the bleachers.

"Be with you guys in a minute," he said.

Maggie, meanwhile, ignored the Hardys and kept training the dolphin. Frank noticed then that she wasn't training Kalea, but another dolphin who was in the lagoon with him.

"Who's that with Kalea?" he asked Stan. "Is it Maile?"

"Take another look, *brah,*" Stan said with a wide smile. "That's Poipu, more or less fully recovered. We let him out of containment just this morning. Maggie's trying to get him back up to speed with a little training. Maile's there, too. Dr. Finski's coming today to pick her up and make her get back to work!"

While Stan finished up his chores, Frank and Joe approached Maggie. The researcher nodded a curt hello and held out her arms in a series of gestures for Poipu. Frank noticed that Poipu watched

Maggie's instructions and then dove underwater for several long moments.

"What's he doing down there?" Frank asked Maggie.

Grudgingly Maggie answered him. "I've got a video rolling down there. Poipu's trained to respond to my hand signals and the video images."

The Hardys watched Maggie and Poipu for a few minutes. Then Joe said, "That's a nice bike we saw out front. It is yours?"

Joe must have caught the researcher off-guard, because Maggie's face brightened for a moment. She scratched the side of her freckled nose and said, "Yes, it is. I've always liked to drive fast, so a bike seemed like the way to go. So?"

"Did you ride it to work yesterday?" Frank asked.

Suddenly Maggie's blue eyes clouded over, and the young woman became defensive again. "Why do you want to know?"

"No particular reason," said Frank.

"Actually I did." Poipu came up out of the water with a hoop in his mouth. Maggie took it from him and then tossed it back into the lagoon. After another series of gestures, one of which Frank recognized from the day before, Maggie went on. "The funny thing was, when I went to grab lunch, it was gone from the parking lot. I think someone took it for a joyride or something, because a few hours later it was back in the lot. Weird, huh?"

"Very," Joe agreed, giving Frank a look.

Frank decided to try another tack. "We're starting to think Jack may have actually been looking for the treasure when he disappeared. Do you know anything about that?"

For one brief moment Frank thought he detected a guilty look pass over Maggie's tanned face. Then the young researcher shook her short red-blond hair and said, "No, I don't. Jack was a researcher. He had a promising career in front of him. Why would he chuck it all for some stupid treasure, even if there is a big reward?"

Frank pursued the line of questioning. "So you know about the reward?"

Maggie's blue eyes shifted uncomfortably. "Sure I do. Doesn't everyone in Nai'a Bay? It's pretty common knowledge, wouldn't you say?"

"If you know about the treasure," Joe said.

At the side of the lagoon, Poipu squealed for Maggie's attention. Looking relieved at the distraction, Maggie said to Frank and Joe, "I'm pretty busy right now. I really don't have time for this."

Frank realized they weren't going to get much more out of Maggie for now. "Okay," he agreed. Then he said to her, "Is Poipu in good enough shape to be back in training?"

Maggie gave Poipu another series of hand signals. "He recovered remarkably well. The vet's going to examine him this morning, but we expect a clean bill of health."

Dr. Cho strolled over, her hands tucked into the pockets of her jeans. "I got your message," she said. "Nothing's come in yet, but do you want to call your friend back in Bayport?"

96

"That's a good idea," Joe agreed. "I'll be right back," he told Frank, and then he followed Dr. Cho back inside.

Alone, Frank watched Maggie put Poipu through his paces. After watching the researcher's hand signals for several minutes, Frank remembered the gesture he recognized from the day before. When Maggie held her hand to her forehead, as if she were saluting, that meant Poipu was supposed to find something. Maggie put down the hoop and held out a small metal box for Poipu to see. She tossed the box into the lagoon and gave Poipu the "find" command again. Then she shaped her hands into a square. Obviously Poipu was supposed to find the box. After swimming around the lagoon for several minutes, Poipu came up from the bottom, pushing the box before him. Maggie clapped, kissed Poipu on the nose, and tossed him a fish for a reward.

Next, Maggie gave Poipu the salute and pointed at the video camera below the water. Curious, Frank knelt to the water level and was barely able to make out the image on the video screen.

"What are you doing?" Maggie demanded when she saw Frank looking at the video.

"Just watching," Frank insisted.

"You're not supposed to be here when we're training the dolphins," Maggie stated flatly. "Do you mind?"

"That's a new rule to me," said Frank, "but okay. I'll go."

He sat in the bleachers, keeping his eyes on

97

Maggie. The image he'd seen on the video screen was familiar, and Frank had a hunch about what Maggie was training Poipu to find. After a few minutes, Joe returned. Frank motioned for his brother to join him.

"Guess what I just saw," Frank whispered.

"I give up," said Joe. "What?"

Frank explained to Joe about Maggie telling Poipu to find the hoop and then the box.

"So?" Joe said. "Big deal."

"It is a big deal," Frank said. "When you find out what she's training Poipu to look for now. Or actually I should say *who*."

"Who?" Joe asked.

"Our friend, and hers—Jack Storm."

# 11 A Deadly
# Scuba Dive

Joe let the news sink in. "How do you know?" he asked.

Joe listened as Frank explained what he had seen. "I recognized Jack from one of the pictures on his fridge. He's wearing a scuba outfit in the video, but his eyes are unmistakable." He reminded Joe about Jack's unusual hazel eyes and his penetrating gaze. "It's got to be him."

Joe looked down at the lagoon from the bleachers. Maggie was tossing the metal box into the lagoon, giving Poipu instructions to find it.

"So she's training him to find the treasure, too!" Joe exclaimed. "She obviously got here early to give Poipu some special training before Dr. Cho showed up. She probably didn't think you'd recognize Jack on the videotape."

99

"Exactly," said Frank. "And my guess is, she's been dying for Poipu to get better so she can swim out with him and find Jack. After all, Poipu probably saw Jack last."

"Too bad," Joe said. He shot his brother a rueful grin. "We're about to spoil her plan."

"What did you have in mind?" Frank asked.

Joe stood up. "If Maggie can take Poipu out to find Jack, then so could someone else."

"Such as?" Frank asked.

"Frank and Joe Hardy!" Joe announced. "Ready for a crash course in dolphin training?"

Frank smiled. "You bet I am."

Joe climbed down from the bleachers and motioned to Stan, who was putting the hose back in place, to follow them.

"What's up?" Stan wanted to know, once they were inside the center.

"We think Maggie is training Poipu to find Jack and the treasure," Joe stated flatly.

"No way!" Stan's brown eyes widened in surprise. He glanced over his shoulder out at the lagoon where Maggie was still instructing Poipu. "What makes you say that?" he asked, turning his gaze back to the Hardys.

Joe explained how Frank had recognized Jack on the video monitor, and that he'd also seen Maggie training Poipu to fetch a box. "If Dr. Cho says it's okay, can you take us out with Poipu?" Joe asked. "Do you know the signals well enough to get Poipu to look for Jack?"

"I think so." Stan's expression was serious. "But we'll have to show him an image of Jack out on the boat to reinforce the command."

"We'll put a VCR and a monitor on the boat," said Frank. "I can hook something up to get us the electricity to keep it running."

"It's a plan," Joe said in excitement. "Let's just hope Dr. Cho will go along with it."

On the way to Dr. Cho's office, Frank asked Joe about the news from Con Riley. Joe told his brother that the detective still hadn't gotten any results from his search on Jack's fingerprints.

"Con said he's going to keep trying until he turns something up," Joe said.

Stan stopped in his tracks. "You guys think Jack and Maggie are crooks, don't you?"

Joe saw the look of dismay on Stan's face. "We don't know," he replied truthfully. "But we suspect that Jack might have been looking for the treasure."

"And that now Maggie is looking for both Jack and the treasure," Frank added.

Stan let out a deep sigh and started walking down the hall again. "That would stink," he said, "if Jack was using Poipu to find the treasure."

"Of course!" Joe cried. "All this time, we never put the two pieces together. Jack must have trained Poipu to look for the treasure. That's why he was taking him out for those swims!"

"We still face a problem," said Frank.

"Which is?" Joe asked.

"Where *is* Jack Storm, and does he have the treasure?" Frank said. "Is it possible that he found the treasure and took off?"

"Maggie doesn't seem to think so," Joe pointed out. "Or else she wouldn't be using Poipu to help her find Jack. The key thing is that we get Poipu out before she does. Otherwise, she might find Jack and the treasure. Then the two of them could take off and we'd never solve our mystery!"

By now the Hardys and Stan were in front of Helen Cho's office. Dr. Cho seemed surprised to see Joe back again so soon. She was even more surprised when the Hardys sat down inside her office and explained their suspicions about Maggie and Jack. And that Maggie meant to use Poipu to find Jack—and the treasure, too.

"These are two prized researchers you're talking about," Cho said angrily. "I trust you boys are good at what you do, but it's going to be hard for me to stomach this."

"We could be wrong," Joe said softly. "Let's hope we are. But we can't let a lead like this go by without chasing it down."

Cho leaned back in her chair and folded her arms across her chest. "What did you have in mind?"

"We want to take Poipu out ourselves," Joe said bluntly. "Since Maggie's been training him, we think he can help us find Jack." And the treasure, Joe thought.

Cho's expression clouded over. "Poipu's only just recovered from his wound. It would be dangerous."

"Stan will be with us," Frank said. "At the first sign of trouble, we'll sail right back."

"We're low on scuba gear," Cho countered.

"I can borrow the extra gear from Uncle Billy," Stan said.

"It may be the only way we'll succeed in finding Jack," Joe finished. "So far we haven't had much luck on our own."

"Neither have the police," Dr. Cho observed. The director seemed to be deep in thought for a moment. Faced with the Hardys' enthusiasm, she obviously couldn't hold on to her doubts. "I think it's risky, but I also agree with you that it may be the only way." Cho sighed, looked away, and drummed her fingers on her desk. "Okay," she said finally. "I'll let you do it. But only because I think it's critical that you boys find Jack before Maggie does. If you're right, and the two of them are working together, then the pressure is on to beat Maggie at her own game."

A knock came at the door. Joe turned in his chair to see Jerry Finski standing in the doorway. The researcher's curly hair look uncombed and there were dark circles under his eyes.

"I came to pick up Maile," he told Dr. Cho. "Am I interrupting?"

"Not at all," Cho said. "Come on in." When Finski had sat down, Helen said to him, "Jerry, you look terrible. What's wrong?"

"I didn't sleep all night," Finski admitted, rubbing his tired eyes. "I guess I was worried about Maile, my research, you know."

Cho cleared her throat. "We can talk about that later," she said gently.

Joe got the distinct impression that Dr. Cho didn't want to discuss the matter in front of them. In fact, she changed the subject almost immediately.

"Frank and Joe want to take Poipu out to look for Jack," Cho told Finski.

Finski raised an eyebrow and looked at the Hardys with curiosity. "I guess it could work. Poipu's got the training." Then the researcher stood up, obviously distracted. "I just wanted to stop by and let you know I was here. I'll be around. Call me at my desk when you're ready to talk."

The Hardys spent the next ten minutes in Dr. Cho's office finalizing their plans. As they were leaving, Maggie Cone rushed down the hall. Her face was flushed and her eyes shone brightly.

"Jerry says you're going to let these kids take Poipu out," Maggie said to Dr. Cho.

"That's right," said Cho firmly. "I am. Do you have a problem with that?"

"Actually, I do," Maggie stammered. "Poipu's not ready for open water."

"Then why were you training him for just that?" Joe asked.

"What are you talking about?" Maggie demanded, her face flushing an even deeper red. "Who are you to come here—"

"Hold on just a second." Cho held out her hand. "Maggie, Frank and Joe say you were training Poipu to find Jack and the treasure."

Maggie scowled. "I don't know what you're talking about," she said angrily. "I'm in charge of training Poipu, and that's what I've been doing."

"You showed him a video of Jack on the underwater screen," Joe put in. "You instructed him to find Jack."

"It was experimental," Maggie tried to explain. "I never planned to take him out."

"So what was the point of showing him the image of Jack in the first place?" Frank wanted to know.

"What is this?" Maggie demanded. "Are people guilty until they're proven innocent around here? Gosh, remind me to look for another job!"

With that, the young researcher turned on her heel and stormed off. Dr. Cho sighed. "I never thought I'd see the day when my top people turned out to be liars."

Joe tried to reassure the ICS director. "We'll get to the bottom of this. I promise."

"I hope so." Cho shook their hands and wished them luck. "Please be careful with Poipu. Nothing must happen to jeopardize his health."

"Don't worry," said Stan. "I'll look after him like he was my own brother."

A half hour later, the Hardys were getting ready to sail out from the ICS dock. Stan and Joe had picked up their gear from Uncle Billy's, while Frank rigged the ICS speedboat's battery to run the

VCR and monitor. When Stan and Joe returned with their gear, Jerry Finski stopped by to wish them luck. Maggie was on the dock, too, her eyes narrowed, keenly watching their preparations. Joe could tell the woman was fuming about the fact that they got to take Poipu out instead of her.

As soon as Stan started up the boat, Poipu began to swim out toward the reef. At the back of the boat, Frank kept the VCR cued to the image of Jack in case Poipu needed reinforcement with his training. He also had the box Maggie was using to train Poipu to locate the treasure. Joe stood at the bow of the boat, calling out instructions to Stan.

"He's headed for Devil's Hat," Joe cried. Poipu was speeding through the reef, cutting a beeline for the triangular island. Then the dolphin stopped suddenly and wheeled around to swim beside the boat. "I think he needs reinforcement," Joe told his brother.

Frank propped the TV monitor at the side of the boat. Poipu came toward the screen, squealing and whistling. Stan handed the boat's controls over to Joe, picked up the box beside the VCR, and proceeded to give Poipu a series of hand signals.

"Find Jack," Stan instructed. "Find treasure."

Suddenly the dolphin was off again.

· "That seemed to work," Stan said, grinning.

Up ahead, in the waters around Devil's Hat, Joe spotted Jerry Finski's trawler. Beside it, the MacAllisters' boat cruised the waters. Joe could clearly make out Brad and Dan, hauling in their fishing nets. "Uh-oh," said Joe. "I think we've got trouble."

"What's wrong?" Frank asked from the boat's stern.

Joe pointed out the MacAllisters' boat. "Company," he said. "Let's see if we can avoid them."

But just as Stan was about to cut out of the way of the MacAllisters, Poipu began squealing and whistling—loudly.

"He's found something," Stan said excitedly.

"Let's go!" Joe cried. He reached for his scuba gear at the same time Frank grabbed his own. "If Poipu takes us out to the MacAllisters, then I'm going to confront them once and for all about Jack's disappearance."

Poipu was waiting anxiously by the side of the boat. When Frank and Joe finally submerged themselves, Poipu swam between them, whistling loudly. Joe held on to the dolphin's fin, while Frank tagged along by holding on to Joe's tank. Soon they were all three speeding toward Devil's Hat—and the MacAllisters' boat.

Joe felt his excitement rising. He just knew Poipu was about to help them crack the case. If the dolphin led them to the MacAllisters, then—

Feeling a tug on his tank, Joe turned to find his older brother clutching at his throat. Suddenly Frank was throwing off his scuba tank and swimming to the surface.

What on earth . . . ? Joe thought. Where's he going?

A second later, Joe felt his lungs clench. In that instant he realized what must have happened to his brother. The mixture coming from their scuba tanks was off. While the pain burned his lungs, Joe realized that he had to act fast. If not, the very air he was breathing would kill him!

# 12 Once a Mobley, Always a Mobley

At the surface, Frank clutched his chest and gulped fresh air. In desperation, he looked through the deep blue water. Joe was down there—somewhere—and he was in serious danger.

Frank tossed Stan his scuba tank and regulator. "What are you doing?" Stan asked him.

"I'm going after him!" Frank cried.

Sucking in a deep breath, Frank dove underwater. The ocean was deep, and Frank couldn't see to the bottom. Joe might be down there by now. Frank had to save him—and fast!

Frank swam down, keeping his eyes peeled for a sign of Joe. Soon the reef's sharp points were skinning his hands as he guided himself across the ocean floor. Frank felt his breath running out. Where was Joe? He had to be here somewhere!

Finally Frank spied his brother. Joe was floating in the water. He'd thrown off his regulator, but Frank could see Joe wasn't moving.

Swimming to Joe's aid, Frank swung his arm around his brother's waist. Frank felt as though his lungs were going to explode as he dragged them both to the surface. Ten more feet, and then fresh air. Five, now four, three, two, one.

"Eayaah!" Frank cried out, gasping, as he broke through to the surface. "Over here!"

A second later, Stan had the boat by their side. Frank passed Joe over to Stan, who hoisted him up and into the boat. Frank was there a moment later, bending over Joe and calling out his name.

"Joe!" Frank cried. "Wake up, bro. It's me, Frank. Joe—can you hear me?"

Frank leaned over and started giving his brother mouth-to-mouth resuscitation. One, two, three, Frank counted as he breathed. Then he removed his lips and pressed down on Joe's chest. Frank was about to try again when suddenly Joe sputtered, blowing out a fountain of water. The younger Hardy coughed, and his eyes fluttered open.

"What happened?" Joe wanted to know.

"Our scuba tanks malfunctioned," Frank told him. "Not enough oxygen in the mixture."

"Uncle Billy," Joe mumbled. He tried sitting up, but quickly sank back down again and closed his eyes. "That hurts," he said.

"What does?" Stan asked.

"Everything. My head, my neck. The works." Joe

blinked several times and grimaced. "Wait till I get my hands on that nutcase."

Over the side of the boat, Frank noticed Poipu, flapping the water with his tail. "I think he's wondering what happened to us," he told Stan.

"Party's over," Stan called out to Poipu. He started up the boat and turned them back to shore. "Time to head in. First of all, there's no way we can use your scuba gear. Second of all—check out the weather."

Clouds were forming, dark and thick, over the West Maui Mountains. Frank thought about his parents, hiking up the volcano. They were sure to get caught in the storm.

"How long will it last?" Frank asked Stan.

Stan scanned the skies, then frowned. "Hard to tell. Rain like this can last two hours or two days."

Joe was struggling to get up again. Frank eased his brother to his feet, then made him sit on one of the benches built into the side of the boat. He popped open a soda from the cooler they'd brought along. Joe took a long drink, then shook his head.

"Will we ever solve this mystery?" he said wanly. "Or will we just keep getting lost at sea?"

Frank laughed. "You're cracking jokes. That's a good sign."

"I guess." Joe rubbed the back of his neck. "I still have a wicked headache, though. The last thing I remember was throwing off my tank, like you did. Then everything went black."

"At least you got rid of the tank in time," Frank said. "Your headache is from the oxygen deprivation. Another thirty seconds—"

"Don't say it," Joe said with a groan. "I thought this was supposed to be a mellow vacation. What happened to sitting on the beach, doing a little surfing, catching a few rays?"

"You want to quit?" Frank asked him.

Joe shook his head firmly. "No way. I want to catch the creep who keeps trying to get us. And I want to find Jack Storm. At this point, do you think I'd leave Hawaii without meeting the guy?"

Within ten minutes, they were back at ICS. Stan guided the boat to the dock. Poipu swam off into the lagoon area. The three boys unloaded the boat. They were just finishing up when the storm began. Sheets of rain soaked them through as they ran from the dock into the Center. There, a group of tourists stared glumly out at the lagoon area. The dolphins were enjoying the rain, but Frank could tell the tourists were disappointed. There was no way they'd be able to swim with the mammals now.

Frank and Joe were both carrying the scuba gear they'd rented from Uncle Billy. "Let's drop this stuff in the jeep—"

"The jeep!" Joe cried.

Out in the parking lot, the jeep was slowly filling with rainwater. While the rain soaked them both, Frank and Joe worked to cover the vehicle with a tarp Frank found in the storage area behind the backseat. Then they both raced back inside the center. Stan was waiting for them with a wide smile on his face.

"Welcome to Hawaii," he said. "Land of enchantment. And rain. I've got a couple of dry T-shirts if you want to borrow some."

Frank's wet shirt clung to him. "How about some shorts, too?"

"No problem, *brah*," said Stan. "I'll outfit you in the full ICS uniform."

Stan led them to the employee locker room. Ten minutes later, Frank and Joe were both dressed in matching blue and white ICS T-shirts and shorts.

"I want to stop by Dr. Cho's office to see if anything's come in from Con yet," Frank told his brother. "Then let's see if we can get through all this rain to Uncle Billy's."

Joe's face was set with determination. "Good. I can't wait to find out what he thought he was doing by sabotaging our scuba gear."

Frank and Joe headed to Dr. Cho's office. The director wasn't in, but Maizie informed Frank and Joe that nothing had come in for them on the fax machine. After telling Maizie where they were going, the Hardys made their way out of ICS and toward their wet jeep.

While Joe drove, Frank watched the rain pour down on the mountain. "Do you really think Uncle Billy wants to keep us away from Devil's Hat?" Frank asked his brother.

"Why else would he sabotage our tanks?" Joe

wondered. "I still think he purposely made us run out of gas last night."

"And that he was the one to shoot at our boat?" Frank asked. "I'm not sure if I believe that. I'm inclined to think it was Brad and Dan."

"How could Brad and Dan have messed with our scuba gear?" Joe asked, taking the road into Nai'a Bay. "Answer me that."

"I can't," Frank admitted. "And I can't explain how they might have snatched Maggie's motorcycle and run us down either. Was that Uncle Billy, too, according to your theory?"

Joe made a face. "I know I was practicing my dirty looks for the MacAllister brothers the other day, but that one was just for you."

The sign on Uncle Billy's shop read Gone Fishing. When Joe saw it, he snorted. "Yeah, right. In this weather?" Then the younger Hardy rapped on the door. After a few loud knocks, Frank heard Billy inside.

"Can't you read the sign?" the man called out. A moment later, he was at the door. When he saw Frank and Joe, he raised his eyebrows. "You boys back so soon? Did the weather get ya?"

"Surprised to see us, huh?" Joe demanded, pushing his way past Uncle Billy.

Frank followed his brother inside the scuba shop. There, Uncle Billy stood with his arms held aloft. "What gives?" the man asked.

"That's what we wanted to know ourselves," said Frank. He held out the scuba gear Joe had rented from the man. "This equipment of yours nearly killed us just now."

Billy's sunburnt face registered surprise. He stepped toward Frank and took the gear from him. "What happened?" he asked.

"The regulators must have jammed," Joe told him. "We stopped getting oxygen out of them."

"You're kidding," Billy said. He checked the regulators, then looked up at Frank and Joe. "Nothing leaves this shop unless it's in tip-top working order. Someone must have jimmied them between here and there."

"Fat chance," Joe said. "We think you did it."

"Me?" Uncle Billy exclaimed. "Why would I do something like that?"

"To keep us off the track of the treasure at Devil's Hat," Frank put in. He leaned against the counter and scrutinized Uncle Billy. It was just a theory, but why else would Billy have fooled with their scuba tanks?

The man's expression seemed to be one of genuine surprise. Suddenly his booming laugh was filling the room and Billy was slapping his knee. "That's a good one," he cried. "You boys think I'd try to kill you just to stop you from doing a little diving around Devil's Hat? Guess again."

Joe looked uncomfortable. "You drew that gun on us the very first day we were in here."

"That was a joke," Billy insisted. "I can see your sense of humor is pretty thin."

"Trying to kill someone isn't very funny," Joe

115

insisted. "How about letting us run out of gas last night?"

"What?" Uncle Billy exclaimed. "You think that was my fault, too?" The man scratched his bushy white beard. "I hate to say it, but I don't think you kids are very good detectives. You ran out of gas, pure and simple. The gauge on that boat was busted. I replaced it myself this morning." He gestured around his shop. "Look, this may seem like a run-down old place, but I try to keep things up. If I rented out lousy stuff, wouldn't I lose my business—fast? And if I've been trying to harm you by giving you faulty regulators, wouldn't that be pretty obvious? You'd trace it back to me right away—like you did—and I'd not only be out of business, I'd be in jail."

Frank realized the man had a point. He had a feeling Billy was telling the truth. If so, that meant someone else had the opportunity to tamper with their equipment. Then he remembered that Maggie had been on the dock when they were loading the boat. It was possible that she had jammed the regulators then. Frank had not been watching the equipment every moment. He hadn't thought he needed to.

Joe was asking Billy about Brad and Dan. "So now you think it's the MacAllisters who are after you?" Billy asked skeptically.

"Someone shot at our boat last night," Joe informed the man. "If that wasn't you, who was it?"

Billy shrugged. "Could have been Brad and Dan, but not because of that treasure," he told them.

"Why not?" Frank asked.

"Brad and Dan MacAllister are fishermen," Billy stated simply. "They don't have any interest in that treasure. They wouldn't care if you looked high and low for it. In fact, they think it's a hoot that I haven't given up all these years."

Frank stored the information. If Billy was telling the truth, they were back to square one as far as the mystery was concerned. Frank saw the look of frustration on Joe's face and realized that Joe was coming to the same conclusion. The phone rang and Billy went to answer it.

"For you," he called out from behind the counter. "It's Dr. Cho."

Frank raced for the phone. On the other end came Helen Cho's voice. "We just got a fax from your friend Con Riley."

"And?" Frank asked.

Cho cleared her throat. "It looks like Jack had a record. He was arrested once for petty theft back when he was in high school."

Frank scratched the back of his neck. "That's not too awful. He probably got in with the wrong crowd."

"Maybe." Dr. Cho sounded distracted. "There's something else," she said.

"What?" Frank asked.

"According to police records, his real name wasn't Jack Storm," Cho said.

Frank motioned for Joe to come over. "It wasn't?" he asked.

"No." Cho paused. "Actually, his name was Jack Mobley."

"But that means—" Frank started.

Cho finished for him. "He was related to Hank Mobley. His father was, in fact, Hank Mobley. The Hawaii Heist thief."

# 13 Poipu
# Disappears

Joe Hardy couldn't believe what his brother was telling him. "Jack Storm is really the son of Hank Mobley, the thief whose treasure is buried somewhere off Devil's Hat?"

"None other," Frank confirmed. "If Con's search is accurate, which I'm sure it is, then we've got a very interesting development on our hands."

"That rascal!" Uncle Billy exclaimed. "He was searching for his father's loot the whole time!" Billy started pacing his shop. "When I think about how I helped him, why, if I get my hands on him, I'll show him what for. Jack Storm, huh? All the while he was really Jack Mobley!"

Joe and Frank left Uncle Billy to ponder the news. Joe wanted to get back to ICS and look at the fax from Con. Outside, it looked as though the rain

119

might be letting up a bit. The clouds were moving south now, and the sky in the west over the mountains almost looked clear. Frank made a quick stop in Nai'a Bay to pick up lunch, and then headed on out to ICS.

While Frank drove, Joe started to put the pieces into place. "So Jack really was after the treasure. Maggie must have been helping him, or at least she knew about it. She's probably been worried this whole time about where he disappeared to. He might even have found the treasure and run out on her."

"I'd buy that theory," said Frank, "except for the fact that Poipu got wounded somehow. Maggie could be worried that something worse has happened to Jack. She doesn't seem to think Jack's left Nai'a Bay. Otherwise, why would she want to take Poipu out to look for him?" Frank made a turn onto the road to ICS. "Besides, even if we could figure out what happened to Jack, we still have the problem of who shot at us that night, and who tried to run you down yesterday."

"And who sabotaged our tanks," said Joe. "Did it ever occur to you that Maggie was lying about someone snitching her bike?" he asked. "What if that was really her trying to run us down?"

"Doubtful," Frank stated. "It would be too incriminating to run someone down on your own bike, don't you think?"

Joe frowned. "You're right." He rubbed his eyes and listened to the sound of the wipers squeaking across the windshield. "There's still too much here that doesn't fit. Who shot at us on the boat? Was that Maggie? Did she follow us out to Devil's Hat? If she didn't run us down, then who did? Was it the same person who shot at us?"

"Don't sound so frustrated," Frank said reassuringly. They were pulling into the parking lot at ICS. "There's Maggie's motorcycle. That means she's here. We'll confront her once and for all with our suspicions."

"And hope she tells us the truth," Joe said glumly.

The door to Cho's office was closed and Maizie Baldwin was nowhere in sight. Joe knocked on the door, only to hear Dr. Cho call out, "I'll be free in ten minutes."

Down the hall, Frank discovered a small company lunchroom, and while he and Joe waited for Dr. Cho to be available, they ate their lunch of teriyaki chicken and fried rice. Ten minutes later, they were back in front of Dr. Cho's office. The door was half-open now, and Jerry Finski stood in the doorway. His back was to Frank and Joe. Since the door was partially closed, Dr. Cho couldn't see the Hardys either.

"Please reconsider," Finski was saying. "I need Maile to finish my research."

"And I'm telling you, I won't let you take Maile out again until you prove to me your research is valid. I need those reports. You said you'd have them for me today. That was our deal, Jerry."

121

"I know," Finski said. "I told you—I'm still crunching the numbers. I'll have the report for you by the end of the week."

"No dice." Helen Cho was firm. "I've given you enough warning. The center has only limited funds. We can't continue research without results. If you can't give me the numbers, we can't keep giving you the funds. And I won't support your keeping Maile out there until you can prove the research is viable."

"It's because of Jack, isn't it?" Finski's voice was raised in anger now. "Why should I pay for another guy's mistakes? Or for the fact that he was willing to endanger Poipu by searching for that treasure?"

Cho's voice was now raised in anger, too. "That's not the issue. Some idiot shot at Poipu. I can't risk that with Maile. So yes, it is because of Jack, but not for the reasons you think. Now, if you'll excuse me, I think we've discussed this long enough."

"Fine," Finski said, and he turned to leave. He spotted Frank and Joe standing outside Cho's office. "Hey, kids," he said brightly, but Joe could see an angry flush coloring his face. "How's it going?"

"Okay," said Joe. "We may have gotten a big break in our case."

"Is that so?" Finski asked, curious. "Getting any closer to finding Jack?"

"If we do, you'll know," Frank told him.

The researcher walked away with a wave. "Keep me posted," he called out.

Joe watched the man leave, then said to his brother, "Finski's got a lot to gain if we solve the mystery. Once we do, maybe Dr. Cho will let him take Maile out again."

"Or maybe not," Frank replied, his voice low. "From the sound of that conversation just now, it seems like he's close to having his research canceled anyway."

Dr. Cho came out from behind her desk and called the Hardys into her office. She picked up two pieces of paper from beside a fax machine and handed them over to Joe.

"Here's what you're looking for," she told them.

Joe quickly scanned the first page. There was a mug shot of a very young Jack Storm. The nameplate below his face read Jack Mobley. Then there was also a more recent photograph that appeared on his California driver's license. The name there read Jack Storm.

"Con's good," Joe said with a low whistle. "He must have had to go back pretty far to find this guy."

The second page contained the facts from Jack's original rap sheet. "It says here that Jack was picked up for shoplifting when he was nineteen," Joe told his brother. "Back then, his name was still Mobley. By the time he was twenty-five, he was going by the name Storm. Con's records show he changed it legally, though. I guess he didn't want to be connected to his father."

"Until now," said Frank. He read the page over Joe's shoulder. "If Jack went to all that trouble to hide who he was, why did he risk giving himself away by searching for his father's lost treasure?"

"Good question," Cho said. Her face was a mask of worry. "This whole time, we've assumed Jack would give up his promising career for a box of jewels. I still have a problem thinking I misjudged Jack. Why would he throw away years of graduate school, all that education and training? It just doesn't make sense."

"Maybe Maggie put him up to it," Joe suggested. "What if he told her who he was, and she convinced him to look for the treasure?"

"That assumes Maggie is greedy as well," Frank put in. "We know she's reckless—"

"But Jack wasn't the type to be convinced of anything," Dr. Cho said. Her almond-shaped eyes narrowed. "There's more going on here. I just wish I knew what!"

"I think Poipu could help us out," said Joe. "Could we try taking him out again?"

Cho frowned and went to look out the window. Joe could tell the rain had stopped even though the skies were still cloudy.

"It seems to be clearing up," the ICS director admitted reluctantly. "Let's get the boat ready, and when the clouds have really parted, yes—I'll let you go."

"All right!" Joe cried. "This time you can be sure I'm going to check our gear myself."

Dr. Cho and the Hardys headed out to the lagoon area. The museum visitors were slowly making their way back outside now that the downpour had ended. Meanwhile, Stan was frantically pacing back

124

and forth at the edge of the lagoon, his brow furrowed.

"What's wrong?" Dr. Cho asked him.

Stan turned to face his boss, surprised. Unless Joe was wrong, there was also some fear mixed in with his expression.

"I—I think we've got a problem," Stan stammered. "I'm sorry. I went on my lunch break, and when I came back—that's when I noticed."

"What?" Frank asked.

"Poipu!" Stan exclaimed. "He's gone!"

Joe's eyes searched the lagoon, and he only saw two dolphins.

Stan bit on his lower lip. "That's not all. . . ."

"What is it?" Joe asked, an awful suspicion coming over him.

"I tried to find Maggie to tell her about Poipu," said Stan. "I thought maybe she saw him go. But she's missing, too. I think she's the one who took him!"

# 14 Danger at Devil's Hat

Frank scanned the open water for some sign of Maggie or Poipu. But from ICS clear to Devil's Hat, the ocean was an empty expanse of blue.

"How are we going to find them?" Joe said with a wail.

"They must have disappeared around the other side of Devil's Hat," Frank remarked. "Where else could they be? If we take Kalea out with the speedboat, I'm sure we can catch Maggie and Poipu!"

Dr. Cho stared helplessly out at the triangular island. "You think they've gone out there," she said quietly.

"We searched the waters around Devil's Hat," Frank said. "We didn't see any sign of Jack. But Maggie seems to think Poipu can find him. Since

126

she's disappeared in open water, it's a logical conclusion that she's around the other side of Devil's Hat."

Cho sighed. "I guess you're right. I'll get Kalea ready. If he's going to follow Poipu, I want to reinforce his training."

While Frank, Joe, and Stan outfitted the ICS speedboat and put together their scuba gear, Dr. Cho went off to work with Kalea. Stan managed to find regulators and tanks for the two of them so they wouldn't have to rent their gear from Uncle Billy. On the dock were several extra tanks and suits.

"Jerry must have brought this equipment back with him when he came in today," Stan said. "I guess he left it here when he went back out."

"So Finski left?" Joe asked.

Stan shrugged. "I was so upset about Maggie, I didn't notice him go. But he must have. His dinghy's gone."

"I don't see him out in the water," Joe said.

"That thing makes good time," Stan told him. "He's probably already at his boat by now."

Frank was impatient to leave, but Dr. Cho was still training Kalea. Frank went to watch her work. Cho was playing a recording of dolphin squeals and whistles through the loudspeakers around the lagoon. In the pauses between whistles, Kalea was trying to mimic the sounds. Dr. Cho saw Frank approach, and then explained the training to him.

"Each dolphin has a unique whistle—a set of sounds all his, or her, own." Cho tossed Kalea a fish and went to replay the tape. "This recording contains Poipu's whistles. I'm training Kalea to imitate them. When Poipu hears his own whistle coming from Kalea, he'll respond. Kalea should be able to find him that way." Cho smiled. "That's one way dolphins echolocate with one another—by imitating each other. That's also one way they distinguish between other dolphins, and something the same size but from a different species—like a shark, for example."

"Dolphins are pretty cool," Frank said.

"I think so," Cho agreed with a smile. "Kalea's ready when you are," she told Frank. "Please be careful. I'd be heartbroken if anything happened to either Kalea or Poipu. Or to you, Joe, or Stan for that matter."

Dr. Cho walked with Frank back to the dock. There, Stan and Joe had just finished loading up the boat. They were both dressed in scuba gear, and Frank donned a suit himself. From the shed where the gear was kept, Joe retrieved a speargun. "This time I'm bringing along backup," he said.

Cho closed her eyes and let out a long breath. "I suppose you need it," she admitted. "Whoever thought such a peaceful place could become so dangerous?"

Stan started up the speedboat. Frank and Joe hopped on board. Dr. Cho called Kalea over to the dock and gave him a series of commands. In a flash, the dolphin was off, speeding through the lagoon toward the reef.

"Let's do it!" Frank cried.

Joe steered them away from the dock, and Cho gave them a wave in farewell. "Good luck!"

Soon they were out in the lagoon, speeding along behind Kalea. The sun was just beginning to appear from behind the clouds, but the water was still a bit choppy from the storm. Frank was amazed at Kalea's instincts. Devil's Hat wasn't that far away, but if Stan was right, and Maggie and Poipu were around the other side, then Kalea's ability to echolocate was keen. The dolphin returned to the boat a few times, with what Frank thought was a questioning look in its eyes. But each time Stan played a tape of Poipu's whistles, and Kalea, imitating the sounds, returned to his search.

The closer they got to Devil's Hat, the more insistent Kalea's calls became.

"We're getting closer," Stan called from the prow of the boat.

Frank was in the stern, double-checking their equipment and loading the speargun. His eyes scanned the dense forest on Devil's Hat and he wondered if perhaps Jack had been hiding on the island the whole time. He could have used Devil's Hat as his base of operation while he searched the waters around it. They should search the island itself next, he decided. His excitement rose as they rounded the southern shore, and so did his fear.

Finski's trawler was out in the waters on the ocean side of Devil's Hat, and so was another.

"Is that Brad and Dan?" Frank asked Joe.

Joe Hardy shifted the speedboat into neutral,

129

surprising Kalea, who wheeled around with a sharp whistle, followed by a complaining squeal.

"Sorry, *brah*," Joe told the dolphin. "You're going to have to tow us the rest of the way."

Frank understood his brother's point. Joe was steering their boat into a protected cove. "If Kalea wants to take us out there, we'll have to sneak up on them."

"I know Uncle Billy said Brad and Dan are only fishermen," Joe said. "But if that's their boat, and Kalea thinks Poipu is out near them, I'm ready to take precautions."

"I agree," said Frank.

"What's the plan?" Stan asked.

Frank was already putting on his scuba tank. "We'll let Kalea guide us. Can you tell what's going on out there?"

Before Joe guided them out of sight completely, Stan took out a pair of binoculars from his duffel bag. He smiled and said, "This time I came prepared." He held the glasses to his eyes. "There's definitely another dolphin out there. I can see the splashing. And there's a diver, too!" he cried.

"Is it Maggie?" Frank asked.

"Hard to say. It could be a woman." Stan squinted. "But it could be a man."

"Let me see," Joe urged, giving Stan the wheel and reaching for the binoculars.

Frank finished putting on his gear while Joe followed the diver with the binoculars. "I can't tell what's going on. It looks like Finski's boat is moored, but the other one is under sail. They're heading north."

"Is the diver with them?" Frank asked.

"I can't tell," said Joe.

Suddenly Frank realized there was a possibility that the MacAllisters had been working with Maggie and Jack this whole time. Maybe the diver was Maggie, and they were all taking a last sail around the waters, knowing that Frank and Joe were on to them. Then Frank remembered how gleeful Brad and Dan had been when Jack turned up missing, and he instantly dismissed the theory that they were working together. The only way to find out would be to ride out with Kalea and learn what was happening firsthand.

By now, Stan had piloted them into the cove, out of sight. The MacAllisters' trawler was still headed north, out of the waters surrounding Devil's Hat. Finski's boat remained moored. Frank could see that the dolphin and the diver stayed close to Finski's boat. He pointed this out to Joe, who squinted in the direction of the ICS trawler.

"You don't think—" Joe began.

Suddenly Frank remembered something he'd overheard in the conversation between Dr. Cho and Jerry Finski. Finski had mentioned Jack's search for the treasure. But unless Frank was wrong, no one had ever told Jerry that Jack was looking for the jewels. Then Frank remembered that Finski was on the dock when Joe had had his scuba accident. And Finski was the one to discover Jack's ruined dinghy.

131

Could Finski have been the one to shoot at their boat, too? The whole time Finski had been trawling the waters, Frank and Joe had never thought that the researcher could be responsible for Jack's disappearance. Or looking for the treasure, Frank realized with an awful thought.

Joe had his scuba gear on. Just before Joe got ready to lower himself over the side of the boat, Frank shared his insights with his brother.

"Now who's got the crazy theory?" Joe asked.

"Think about it," Frank said, his mind racing ahead. "Finski could be using Maile to find the treasure. Maybe that's why he's upset about his research being canceled."

"So who's out swimming by his boat now?" Joe wondered aloud, pointing to the dolphin and the diver. "Maggie? Is she his accomplice?"

"I don't know," Frank admitted. "But we'd better find out." He lowered his goggles, gave Joe the thumbs-up, and tumbled over the side of the boat.

Kalea was waiting underwater. As soon as Joe was with them, Kalea swam between Frank's legs. Frank felt Joe grab for his shoulder and hold on tight. And then they were off!

Frank held on to the dolphin's back as Kalea swam through the clear waters. Frank knew that visibility was pretty good. They weren't exactly going to be able to sneak up on the diver. They had to be ready for the possibility of an underwater chase. Luckily Joe had the speargun. Even though he hoped Joe wouldn't have to fire the gun, at least he could use it to scare the diver.

132

His heart beating fast, Frank let Kalea pull them along. Towing two people was hard work for the dolphin. They went slowly enough so that Frank wished he could have appreciated all the underwater life swimming in and around the lush coral reef. But his mind wasn't on identifying the schools of brightly colored fish. A sea turtle swam by, close enough for Frank to see its large shell and scaly legs. Angelfish darted past. Sea slugs appeared out of the coral that camouflaged them. But Frank still concentrated on keeping his hands on Kalea's thick fin, and his legs close to the dolphin's wide body.

A shadow appeared in the waters, cast from the surface. Frank looked up to see the outline of the fishing trawler. They were close! The diver had to be around here somewhere. In the still waters ahead, Frank saw a cloud of sand. Only another diver could stir up the waters like that.

He motioned to Joe. Frank felt his brother stiffen. With even sharper whistles, Kalea swam on, toward the swirling sand. And then—suddenly—they were close enough to see Poipu.

Kalea's whistles pierced the ocean stillness. Poipu answered back, and soon the waters were alive with the two dolphins calling out to each other. Poipu swam toward Kalea.

And then Frank saw the diver.

Surprised to see Poipu swimming off, the diver looked in their direction. No more than ten feet away, Frank could easily see who it was. Behind the goggles, it wasn't Maggie's face peering out at him.

It was Jack Storm.

# 15 Underwater Showdown

Motioning to Joe, Frank warned his brother to back away. They'd need a plan. Otherwise, after spending all this time searching for Jack, he could slip right through their hands. And there was no way Frank was going to let that happen!

Frank eased off Kalea. Joe swam around to Frank's side. When Joe saw the diver, he readied his speargun.

Ready for anything, Frank watched the man's reactions. Jack raised his arms in surrender. And Frank noticed that Storm held a metal box in his right hand. The treasure!

Joe must have realized by now that the diver was Jack. Without waiting for Frank, the younger Hardy swam over to Jack. Joe still had his speargun poised, ready to shoot if necessary.

Frank followed right behind Joe. Beside him, Kalea played with Poipu. The dolphins called out to each other and played underwater tag. By the time Frank got to Jack, Joe was already taking the box from his hand, while he kept the speargun aimed at Jack's chest.

A million questions went through Frank's mind. If Poipu was around, where was Maggie? Where had Jack been this whole time? Why was he giving himself up so easily to the Hardys, especially when he had no idea of who they were? The problem was, he couldn't ask Jack any of these questions since they were underwater.

Jack's face as Frank approached was a mask of worry. His eyes darted back and forth between Frank and Joe, and he was obviously trying to determine if they were planning to hurt him. With Joe's speargun at his chest, Frank wasn't surprised!

Joe was struggling with the box. Jack caught Frank's eye and pointed to the waters overhead. Frank grabbed on to Jack's arm. The only way they were going to get all this settled was to head back to the boat and hash it out.

But Jack shrugged off Frank's hand and went back to pointing overhead. Frank and Joe exchanged a look, at which point Frank realized that Joe was just as frustrated as he was. Again Frank motioned over his shoulder, indicating that they should swim back to their boat. And again Jack pointed overhead.

Joe went on the other side of Jack. It was clear that Frank and Joe were going to have to get Jack back to the ICS speedboat. Between the two of them, they could force him to come with them.

As Frank and Joe dragged Jack, the scientist gestured frantically overhead. As Kalea swam around them, Jack suddenly gestured madly at the dolphin's dorsal fin. Then he pointed up at the shadowed waters overhead once more. Frank and Joe exchanged a puzzled look. What was so important about the dolphin's fin? Suddenly Frank understood. Jack was pointing at the trawler that was anchored above them, and then to Kalea's fin. If Frank was right, Jack's pantomime confirmed his own suspicions.

Fin, fin, *Finski!* Frank thought.

Jack was telling them to beware, that the danger was really coming from Jerry Finski. Joe must have caught on at the same time, because he let go of Jack's arm and scanned the waters overhead, his speargun aimed in that direction.

Frank kept his grip tight on Jack. It could be a trick. But slowly the pieces started falling into place. Finski's trawler was always out in the waters around Devil's Hat. Frank realized that Finski had always had the opportunity, each time Frank and Joe had run into trouble. Not only had Finski been on the ICS dock when their scuba gear malfunctioned, he'd also been at ICS when Joe got run down by the motorcycle rider. In fact, Finski had been standing there when they decided to go to the library to do their research.

If he was right, then Finski had been looking for the treasure all along. And Finski had even been using Maile to help find it. That was probably why he'd been so upset when Dr. Cho decided not to let Maile return to the boat with them.

And if all these theories were right, Jerry Finski was a very dangerous man.

Frank had just finished putting the facts into place when he noticed the telltale bubbles of a scuba diver. A swimmer was heading toward them.

Joe froze. So did Jack. Even Kalea and Poipu became more agitated as they swam around Frank, Joe, and Jack. Frank looked up into the waters overhead to see Jerry Finski heading for them, a speargun in his hand.

Before Frank had a chance to move, Jack was calling out to Poipu with a whistle and giving him a command with his hands. Poipu was there in a flash, and a moment later, Jack had grabbed on to the dolphin's back and was letting him carry him away to safety.

Finski seemed not to know how to react. Neither did Frank or Joe. For an awful instant Frank thought that maybe they'd all been fooled by Jack. And now he was swimming off with the treasure!

As soon as Finski lowered his speargun in Jack's direction, Frank knew his hunch about Finski had been right. Behind his goggles, the expression on the man's face was unmistakable: outright rage at having his plan foiled.

Frank had to do something. Finski was ten feet away, out of arm's reach. But in another second, he would shoot his speargun at Jack!

Just as Frank readied himself to interfere with

the man's deadly move, Joe Hardy lunged at Finski. The move knocked Joe's own speargun from his hand, and Frank watched in horror as the weapon fell through the water. Quickly he swam toward it, but it was too late. The speargun was on its way to the ocean's depths—and now Frank and Joe were unarmed.

There was no time to think about their disadvantage. Joe had Finski in an armhold, and Frank had to do whatever he could to help his brother. While Joe struggled to keep Finski from shooting the speargun, Frank raced to his aid. Swimming toward Finski, Frank could see the barely controlled fury in the man's eyes.

Priming himself for a fight, Frank came at Finski with his fists raised. It wouldn't be easy to knock the man out underwater, Frank knew, but he had to try!

Frank kept his eyes alert for any quick moves. Joe had his arm around the man's neck now, and Finski was struggling to break free. Frank rushed in, seizing an opportunity. He thrust his fist out with all his might, and made contact with Finski's chest. The man weakened a bit, but managed to return the blow with one of his own—a sharp knee into Frank's stomach.

Frank doubled over from the pain, surprised at the man's strength. In that moment of defense, he floated out of Finski's reach—safe for now from another blow. As he recovered, Frank planned his next move. Joe was wrestling with the man's right arm, trying to get the speargun free. But Finski was putting up a good fight. Joe forced the gun over the man's head. Finski countered by yanking it down and to the right, out of Joe's reach. Joe charged the man by throwing both arms around his waist.

Now was the moment. Frank readied himself to come in and deliver a knockout blow.

But Finski caught his eye in that instant and saw Frank's plan. He raised his speargun—barely keeping it out of Joe's reach—aimed, and fired.

Time seemed to pass in slow motion. Frank saw the projectile headed right for him, but it seemed to take forever to make contact. When it did, Frank felt a searing pain in his right arm and sensed the spear pierce his flesh.

And then everything went black.

# 16 Tropical Paradise

Joe Hardy watched in horror as his brother fell through the water, the wound in his upper arm clearly visible through his punctured scuba suit. Finski struggled in Joe's grip, finding a way to break free. In the split second that Joe took to look at his brother, he involuntarily loosened his hold. Finski shrugged off Joe's grip and tore off through the water.

Joe was frustrated. Below him, Frank sank toward the ocean's bottom. But Finski was heading to the safety of his boat. The scientist was going to try to make his escape. Who knew if they'd be able to catch him once he headed away from Devil's Hat?

But Joe had no choice. He had to save his brother. Then, just as he turned from watching Finski, Joe saw an amazing sight. Kalea was diving through the water to rescue Frank! Joe watched in stunned delight as the dolphin swam under Frank, balanced him across his back, and then coasted off in the direction Jack had taken. Joe saw Frank move slightly, and realized in relief that his brother had regained consciousness. As Kalea swam off, Frank grabbed on to Kalea's fin.

Somehow, Kalea knew the safest course! Jack would no doubt spot them and, Joe hoped, would take care of Frank. The ICS boat wasn't too far away. Stan could speed Frank to safety if he was badly injured.

Turning to swim after Finski, Joe clenched his teeth in anger. You're not getting free, Joe thought, not after what you just did to my brother! Joe had a tough fight ahead of him, especially now that Frank couldn't help. But he knew he could do it.

Joe trailed Finski through the clear water. The scientist hadn't gotten much of a lead. Joe was almost within arm's reach of the man's flippers. He lunged, grabbed the rubber, and pulled—hard.

Unfortunately, Joe merely succeeded in coming away with one of Finski's flippers. He stared at the footwear in his hand and scowled. A second later, he tossed the flipper away and swam even harder after the scientist.

This time Joe didn't risk anything. He dug through the water until he was abreast of the scientist. The second Finski saw Joe, he aimed his speargun at him. But in that moment, Joe thrust his leg out at Finski's arm. The blow caught the scientist off guard, and Finski let the speargun fall.

Now we're even, Joe thought.

Propelling himself with all his might, Joe came at the scientist, his fists raised. Joe lashed out at Finski's face, but the water put up too much resistance. By the time the blow made contact, it had as much power as a slap. Joe tried again, and again it felt as if he were moving his hand through mud. His fist jarred Finski, but that was all.

Nothing's working, Joe thought.

For every blow Joe tried to land, Finski was there to defend himself. The man even landed a few decent jabs of his own, despite the underwater resistance.

Joe fought off Finski's blows well enough to get close to the guy. He clutched the man by the shoulders and continued to ward off the jabs Finski sent to Joe's head. Moving his hands close together, Joe tightened his grip. If he could just get his hands around Finski's neck—

He was just about to try throttling the guy when Joe had an idea. In one of his karate magazines, he read about a move involving pressure points. With enough force applied in the right spots, you could actually knock a guy out with your fingertips. There was a spot by the carotid artery. If Joe could just get close enough.

He edged his hands toward the spot under Finski's throat, beside his Adam's apple. The guy was still putting up a fight! Joe had to thrash about to avoid the blows to his head, his chest, his stomach. But the underwater resistance that had been working against Joe when he tried to knock

142

out Finski was working for him now. The man's blows hardly felt like anything by the time Finski pushed his fist through the water!

Closer. A few more inches. Joe felt for the spot, and hoped his memory was correct. At the last moment before Joe applied the pressure, Finski stared at Joe in surprise.

Never thought I'd beat you, huh? Joe thought.

He pressed his fingers deep into the spot. Slowly he felt Finski weaken and then lose control. And in another instant, the man was falling, unconscious, into Joe's arms.

Joe didn't let himself feel relief. He still had to get the guy to the surface before he woke up and started struggling again. Steadily Joe climbed through the clear blue water. Finally he broke the surface. Joe was faced with the problem of what to do with the man, now that he was unconscious.

Joe was struggling for a solution when he heard the whine of a speedboat fast approaching. In another moment the boat was upon them, and Joe looked up to see his brother standing on the deck.

"You're okay!" Joe Hardy cried.

Frank's scuba suit was down around his waist, and his upper arm was bandaged. "The spear pierced the flesh, but it didn't go too deep," Frank yelled.

Finski groaned and moved. Joe kept his grip tight around the man's neck. "Want to help me with this guy?" Joe asked.

"My pleasure," said Frank.

He tossed Joe a life preserver, which Joe threw

over Finski's head. Then, with Joe keeping close behind, Frank hauled the scientist into their speedboat. On deck, Jack and Stan gave hoots of delight as Frank lifted Finski aboard. Maggie was there, too. Just as Joe climbed onto the boat, Finski came to long enough to ask, "Where am I?"

"Right where you belong," Frank Hardy said. "On your way to police custody!"

Stan radioed Dr. Cho, who informed him that she would get in touch with Mike Lam. While Stan cruised them back to ICS, Frank and Joe questioned Jerry Finski about his involvement in the treasure at Devil's Hat.

"It was you who ran into Jack the night of his disappearance, wasn't it?" Frank asked.

When Finski nodded glumly, Jack himself added, "Jerry kept me tied up on his boat. He used me to try to search for the treasure. That's how I ran into you guys down below."

Finski's brown eyes narrowed on the group. The man was fully conscious now. He strained against the rope Joe had used to tie his wrists to the speedboat's railing. "If you kids hadn't gotten involved, my plan would have succeeded. Maile would have found the treasure, with Jack's help, and I would have let him go."

"How did you plan to get away with it?" Joe wanted to know.

"I was going to sail off in that trawler and never be heard from again," Finski said. "What do you think it's like for a scientist, living from grant to

144

grant, job to job? My life was never secure, never certain. My research wasn't getting me rich, that was for sure, and Helen Cho was going to cut me off anyway. I wasn't getting results."

"So you jumped at the lure of the treasure," Frank put in.

"Of course," Finski agreed. "Not at first, not when I first started working at ICS. But over time I began to see finding the treasure was the only way out for me. So I started looking for it at night, on the weekends, that sort of thing. Then I ran into Jack one night, and he gave me the brilliant idea to use the dolphins to locate the treasure. I made a plan: Kidnap Jack, and use him and Poipu to find the box of jewels. Then Poipu got injured—"

"How did that happen?" Maggie asked.

"By accident," Jack said, putting an arm around the young woman. "Finski got me on board his trawler by threatening me with his speargun. I tried to fight back. The gun went off and shot Poipu. I'm glad he managed to get back to ICS."

"You were lucky," Frank said. "Poipu's injury was what tipped us off to the fact that you were in danger in the first place."

By now, Stan was piloting them toward the ICS dock. Dr. Cho was waiting for them when they came ashore. Mike Lam was there, too, along with several squad cars and members of the Nai'a Bay police department. They escorted Finski away, and Frank, Joe, Stan, Jack, and Maggie followed Cho to her office, where they caught each other up on what had gone on out at Devil's Hat.

Cho was stunned to learn that Finski was behind all the trouble from the start. "On the boat ride back to ICS, Finski confessed to his crimes," Joe explained. "He ran into Jack the night of Jack's disappearance—"

"What were you doing out there?" Cho asked Jack. "Are Frank and Joe right? Were you looking for the treasure?"

Jack hung his head and admitted the truth. "I was." His startling hazel eyes filled with sadness and he pushed back the wet brown hair from his forehead. "From the time I was a kid, I was ashamed of what my father had done. When I got here, and learned that it was in Nai'a Bay that my dad went down—and that the treasure was buried here somewhere off Devil's Hat—I promised myself I'd locate this box." Jack clutched the strongbox in his hands. "I wanted to find the jewels and return them to their rightful owners."

Cho looked at Jack sympathetically. "I never thought you had turned into some kind of greedy treasure seeker. I always knew there had to be a logical explanation."

The group was silent for a moment. Maggie reached out to hold Jack's hand, and gave it an affectionate squeeze.

"One thing that's bothered me," Frank put in, "and that's how you were involved, Maggie." He cleared his throat and said, "If you knew about the treasure, why didn't you help us find Jack? Why did you go out on your own with Poipu?"

Maggie's face blushed red. She took a deep breath and said, "I know this doesn't make much sense. But I thought you'd be sure Jack was guilty if I told you anything. I didn't see how I could explain the whole thing to you. I guess I'm so used to solving things by myself that I never thought you could actually help." The words rushed from her and then she paused. "Also, I was afraid you might find out that Jack and I were involved. I didn't know how Helen would feel about that, and we had agreed to keep our relationship a secret. I guess I figured all along that if I could only find Jack, everything would be fine again."

Jack reached out to put his arm around Maggie. "And it is, see?" Then he went to defend his girlfriend. "Maggie's stubborn and headstrong, and that's why I love her. She promised me she'd never tell anyone that I was Hank Mobley's son. Sometimes all her good qualities get her into trouble. Like earlier this afternoon. She swam out with Poipu, but Finski caught her. He tied her up and held her on his boat until we were able to rescue her—right before we came to save Joe."

"I'm sorry if I made it harder on you guys," Maggie apologized.

"That's okay," said Joe. "But you should realize you came pretty close to being a suspect!"

Dr. Cho brought them back on track. "So Finski ran into Jack, and shot at Poipu?"

147

Frank nodded. "Then he held Jack hostage on his boat while he continued to look for the treasure."

"Sometimes he let me out to look," Jack put in. "But he was always on guard, watching me, and he always had his speargun aimed at me in case I tried anything funny."

"How did your watch get in Maile's mouth?" Stan asked. "How did you manage that?"

"One time Finski left me tied up above deck," said Jack. "I had my watch in my pants pocket and I was able to get it out and toss it overboard. Maile was there. I gave her a command to find the watch and take it back to ICS."

"Cool," said Stan. "I knew it was proof you were still alive!"

Cho shook her head sadly. "It will take me a while to accept that the treasure made him so greedy, he'd do anything to find it."

"Including harming whoever got in his way," Frank said. "Unless I'm wrong, Mike will learn that Jerry was the one who sabotaged our tanks, and that he stole Maggie's bike that day and tried to run us down."

Joe laughed suddenly. "The MacAllisters were such jerks, we automatically assumed they were up to no good when we saw them diving." He shook his head. "We sure were wrong about them."

"You're right about that," Frank said. "It must have been Finski who shot at our boat that night we were looking for Jack at Devil's Hat."

Maggie leaned toward Jack and smiled at him. "Aren't you going to open the box?" she asked, indicating the treasure. "After everything that's happened, don't you want to see what's inside?"

Jack shook his head. "Nope. I'm going to call the insurance company and have them come pick it up. After that, I'm going back to my research on dolphins. And Devil's Hat will just be a beautiful island on the horizon!"

# NANCY DREW® MYSTERY STORIES  By Carolyn Keene

# THE HARDY BOYS® SERIES  By Franklin W. Dixon

## LOOK FOR
## AN EXCITING NEW
## HARDY BOYS MYSTERY
## COMING FROM
## MINSTREL® BOOKS
## EVERY OTHER

# STAR TREK®
## ◄GENERATIONS™►

### A Novel by John Vornholt

**Based on STAR TREK GENERATIONS**
Story by Rick Berman & Ronald D. Moore & Brannon Braga
Screenplay by Ronald D. Moore & Brannon Braga

## Available from

POCKET
**BOOKS**

A MINSTREL® BOOK